David Rees lives in Exeter and until recently taught at Exeter University. He is a freelance writer. He has written several novels, most of them about young people, including *In The Tent* and best-selling *The Milkman's On His Way*, both of which have a gay teenager as the central character. In 1978 his novel *The Exeter Blitz* was awarded the Carnegie Medal, and in 1980 he was given The Other Award for his historical novel, *The Green Bough of Liberty*. In 1982 and 1983 he lived in San Francisco, and was Visiting Professor at San José State University; the diary he kept of his Californian life, *A Better Class of Blond*, is also published by the Olive Press.

Out of the Winter Gardens

David Rees

Olive Press

First published in Great Britain in 1984 by
The Olive Press, Flat 2, 92 Great Titchfield Street, London, W1

© 1984 The Olive Press

Second impression 1985

Text and cover design by David Williams

Photoset by A.K.M. Associates (U.K.) Ltd.,
Ajmal House, Hayes Road, Southall, Greater London.
Printed in Great Britain by Photobooks (Bristol) Limited

ISBN 0-946889-03-1

Trade distribution in Scotland, North of England,
Midlands, North Wales and Ireland by
Scottish and Northern Book Distribution,
4th floor, 18 Granby Row, Manchester 1 (061-228 3903)
and 48a, Hamilton Place, Edinburgh 3 (031-225 4950)

Trade distribution in South and
South West of England and South Wales by
Turnaround distribution,
27 Horsell Road, London N5

For Marian Robinson

To travel hopefully is a better thing than to arrive.

R.L. Stevenson, *Virginibus Puerisque*

Author's Note

Alresford is a real place, but I have taken a few liberties with its geography and its history for the purposes of this story. The River Itchen is not so close to the railway line as I have suggested, and the fulling mill is not a derelict ruin, but a rather beautiful private house. The Mid-Hants Railway—the "Watercress Line"— was closed to passenger traffic in 1973, but the stretch between Medstead and Four Marks, Ropley, and Alresford has been re-opened in recent years as a tourist attraction.

The Winter Gardens in Bournemouth is a real concert hall, but the orchestra in this story is not meant to bear any resemblance to any actual orchestra, nor is the harpist, Adrian, a portrait of a real person, living or dead.

1. Some kind of ceremony

In the school holidays I could never sleep through the noise of the eight o'clock train leaving Alresford Station. The first slow puffs of smoke—yes, it was a steam train, on an old line that had been re-opened—were accompanied by tremendous wheezings like a gigantic bellows gasping for air, and they always interrupted my dreams. Often I would lazily lift a corner of the curtain and catch a glimpse of thin smoke scribbled like words over the town and the green hills beyond. The engine was a big toy engine with a tall chimney-stack, and it pulled two ancient coaches, relics of the London and South-Western Railway Company. I used to watch it slowly straining along the line, until it was swallowed in the cutting, smoke billowing out in a ribbon. There its noise changed, and as it speeded up a little, it sounded like some underground animal chittering and burrowing its way through the earth. The white ribbon still fluffed out, and as the train was invisible the fields looked as if they were on fire. It was too far off to see when it came out of the other end of the cutting, but I could still hear it, snorting and sniffling down the track to Itchen Abbas and Winchester.

My mother and I shared a windy house called Tralee, high up on a hill, with my Aunt Bridie and my cousin Nic. My Uncle John was dead and my father left home when I was so young that I had almost no memory of him. I don't know why he left: Mum just got so embarrassed when I asked questions about it that I stopped asking.

Nic, an absent-minded and unpunctual boy, at the age of twelve—I'm four years older than he is—made an arrangement with the engine-driver that the eight o'clock train would not leave Alresford during term-time until he was safely on it. (We both went to the same school in Winchester.) How he managed to do this we were never quite sure, but he had a mania for railways and perhaps the engine-driver liked him for his enthusiasm. I say *the* engine-driver, for there was only one, Mr Bowles, a local Alresford man whom my aunt knew slightly. And there was only one train: when it had discharged Nic and me and the other passengers at Winchester, it waited while Mr Bowles had his breakfast, then it trundled back through Itchen Abbas and Alresford to Ropley, Medstead and Four Marks, and Alton. At Alton Mr Bowles had his elevenses; the train ate coal and drank some water, then they both travelled down to Winchester, just in time for lunch. And so on, and so on, all day. My cousin's arrangement worked very well until school broke up for Easter. He forgot to tell Mr Bowles, and on the first day of the holidays (it was, unluckily, April Fool's Day) the eight o'clock train sat in Alresford Station, spluttering and chortling for twenty minutes. Eventually Mr Bowles concluded that Nic and I must be ill—though on previous occasions of sickness my aunt had always run down to tell him—and set off, after the commuters had grumbled to him that they would be late for work. One of them, Colonel Ramsbottom, an important personage on the Winchester City Council, complained to the authorities, and the result of this was the eight o'clock train left, next term, on the dot.

During the summer holidays Nic could spend all the time he wanted—except when he was required to eat or wash up the dishes, or when it was raining—indulging in his passion for railways. I was getting somewhat old for this kind of thing, but I have to admit that I, too, liked railways, and, even at sixteen, I was willing to accompany him on his expeditions, if I had nothing better to occupy myself with. Alresford Station had enormous sidings, all connected up by an elaborate system of points to the main track, and on the rails—rust-stained, with weeds growing between the sleepers —were dozens of old goods trucks. Some of these had been used to carry produce, some to transport cattle, and two were foreign: *Roma Termini* was painted in faded white on one, and on the other, *Conseil Supérieur de Chemins de Fer*. How railway wagons from Italy and France had ended up at sleepy old Alresford was a mystery we never fathomed.

Though Mr Bowles was the only engine-driver, there were in fact two engines. The second of these usually spent its days in the sidings at Alresford doing nothing, but sometimes it would have its fire lit, and it would burble quietly to itself while it waited for Mr Bowles. After he had had his elevenses at Alton there was usually a good hour and a quarter before he was due to leave on his lunch-time run, so, if the second engine was smoking away, he would come down specially to give it a little practice, presumably to see if it was still in working order. (It was even older than the first engine.) This practice involved shunting the trucks about, and required some highly elaborate manoeuvres on Mr Bowles's part, backing the engine up and down the lines and crossing it over the spider's web of points. The trucks were not always coupled together, and, when this was the case, one tap of the engine cannoned the first truck into the second, which then knocked the third, and so on, down the line, until they were all on the move. This produced a very satisfying clonk-clonk-clonk-clonk noise, and the sight was a bit like an extremely long worm that had got something into its digestive system which it didn't approve of. The engine then snorted down a different track until it passed beyond the last wagon; it would then go into reverse and bang all the trucks back again towards the station. Sometimes it uttered the strangest noises, gurgles of delight accompanied by a rapid spurting of tiny white puffs from its chimney, or long sighs as if its intestines were shuddering with convulsions, though the only visible sign of distress was a thin jet of grey smoke dribbling vertically upwards. What the point of all this was we could never find out; and Mr Bowles, a man of few words, was unhelpful: "Shunting practice," he said. Obviously it was, but why? It always ended up with the trucks being moved to the furthest possible position from where they were to start with; if they were on the thirteenth siding, right on the edge of the embankment, they arrived at last on track number two, next to the main track, and there they waited until the next shunting practice, perhaps a week or a fortnight later.

We usually watched these operations from the level point where the cutting sloped steeply down and started to turn itself into an embankment. There was an old shed here, black with tar and the grime of ages, in which various railway tools were kept, such as the enormous spanner-thing the plate-layer used for tightening up bolts on the rails. We would sit with our backs propped comfortably against the shed wall, watching the trucks being propelled towards us, or lie on the ground, our eyes an inch or two from the rail as the big iron wheels rolled slowly by, the sleepers giving under their weight. I often wondered what it would be like to be tied hand and foot to the track with an express train thundering nearer and nearer: would it be a clean cut or a horrible squelchy mess?

Mr Bowles often let Nic travel with him in the cab of his engine. I went once, but I felt that I was doing something rather childish, and, besides, the cab was very dirty. There were certain sorts of dirt I had no

4

objection to—garden earth for instance—but industrial grime like coal dust got into all the creases and lines of my hands so that when I touched anything shivers went up and down my skin. Then there was the shunting itself. Though it was a nice idea being in a powerful machine that banged a host of smaller objects out of its way, I could not see ahead of us at all, so that the moment of impact invariably took me by surprise and I lost my balance or fell against one sooty thing after another.

When Mr Bowles asked us one day if we would like to go down to Winchester on the twelve fifteen, I declined the invitation. Aunt Bridie made some sandwiches for Nic to take with him, as the train was not due to return to Alresford till three twenty. "Why don't you go too, Michael?" she asked. "I can easily butter some more bread."

"I told you, I don't want to."

"Oh, leave him alone, Mum," Nic said as he put his food in a plastic bag.

"I wish you boys were better friends," Aunt Bridie said, when he had gone. "I suppose you've had a quarrel."

"We never quarrel! I just don't like going in the cab of the engine, that's all. Why doesn't anyone around here believe me?"

"Well, you'll have to amuse yourself after lunch. Nora and I are going to the shops."

When we had eaten I went out to find something to do, thinking I would get to the railway eventually, and watch my cousin's triumphant return to Alresford from the vantage point of the black shed. On the other side of the track was a wide lazy stream that wound its way through flat meadows and marshy land where reeds rustled and bullrushes grew immensely tall. Willows wept into the water, their long fronds trailing in the mud, and a row of silky poplars grew on the bank. When I was Nic's age I'd found this a good place for catching tiddlers, but now it was just pleasant to loaf around and enjoy the peace and quiet, or watch the shallows where there might be a trout, a flick of greeny-grey as it darted downstream. Higher up, near the watercress beds, a derelict old fulling mill straddled the river. Its windows were nailed over with wood, and moss and weeds grew in the roof. The thatch had rotted so badly that the top of one of the walls stood open to the sky. I spent much of my time that afternoon trying to break in, but the Itchen Conservancy had made too good a job of their boarding up. My mother had been in there once when she was a young girl; she said it was damp and very dark inside, and the sound of water racing under the mill was magnified into a cascade that roared like Niagara. I tried at last to climb on to the roof, thinking I might get down the chimney, which was very wide and old-fashioned, but nearly six feet tall though I was and standing on a large water-butt, I was just too short to reach the top of the wall. I gave up, and made my way back to the railway, relieving the irritation of my failure by skimming stones over the stream.

I crossed the track and settled myself down against the shed wall. I was just wondering whether to be really infantile and pick a blade of grass, the sort you cup into your hands and blow on through your thumbs to produce an exceptionally hideous shriek, when I saw someone walking along by the stream, a kid about the same age as me, wearing a dark raincoat and Wellington boots. I took little notice of him until he came right up on to the railway line. He didn't come by the obvious route past me, where it was flat and there was an outline of a path, but he poked himself through the wire fence about ten yards off and clambered up the embankment. He looked at me and I looked at him; he glanced back the way he'd come as if someone was following him, and up the line at the station: then he bent down, picked up a large stone, put it on the rail, and ran off down the other side of the embankment into the bushes.

I sat still for some moments, astonished. My first thought was that it was such a pointless thing to do. Then I felt indignant: he obviously imagined I was of so little account that it didn't matter that I'd seen him. It was only then that I thought of the train. My cousin was on that train; supposing it was derailed! I got to my feet, walked down the line, and picked up the stone. It was really big—heavy and jagged. I threw it down the embankment in the direction the boy had gone. It had just left my hand when I saw his face peering out of a clump of broom. The stone went wide of him, and landed with a splosh in some mud, but he probably thought I had thrown it at him deliberately. I tried to affect a great deal of nonchalance and strolled away, hands in pockets, singing "Oh, Mister Porter, what shall I do?" then sat down again, keeping a wary eye on the bushes. All was still.

I was just beginning to think he had gone when there was a sudden violent movement in the undergrowth, and I tensed, fearing a stone might come flying at me. He climbed up the embankment, looked at me again, and placed on the line—yes, it was!—the very same stone. Then, as before, he ran back down into the broom bushes. He's a stark staring loony, I told myself. The three twenty would soon be here; any minute now it would be leaving Itchen Abbas. There was only one thing to do. I sauntered back, singing the same words, picked up the stone, turned, and gently dropped it down the other side of the embankment. This time he started up the slope before I had moved off, so I went at a quicker pace than before, though nothing so fast that it could be called a run. It's like being part of some kind of ceremony, I thought.

"Oi! Oi, you!"

I stopped. "What do you want?"

He was standing in the middle of the track. "What's your name?"

"Maurice," I said, after some moments wondering if I should reply.

He came towards me until he was quite close. I could see his face properly now and I wasn't at all reassured. It was a fat, red, ugly face with mean, brown eyes. He looked rough as well as mad. He hadn't a shirt on under his raincoat, just a vest, grimy at the neck.

"Maurice what?"

"Maurice Bartlett." (This was a real name; Maurice Bartlett was someone I'd met when we were on holiday in Scotland last summer.)

He was silent, staring. Nothing he could sneer about in that name; it wasn't funny or cissy, and it didn't rhyme with anything soppy.

"How old are you?" he asked.

"Mind your own business."

"You're a liar."

"What?"

"You calling me a liar?" I did not answer. "I said are you calling me a liar?"

"No."

"Well then."

This wasn't getting us very far, I thought. At least he hadn't hit me: he was strong and well-built. I started to walk away.

"Oi! How old are you?"

"Sixteen," I said, wearily.

"You're a bleeding liar. You ain't sixteen."

"How old am I then?"

"Four."

He slithered down the embankment, looking for the stone. It had rolled into a dense patch of brushwood, and he had some difficulty finding it; the ground was wet and slimy too, but this did not deter him. I watched him wrestle with prickly hawthorns and blackberries, and once he skidded on the mud and nearly fell over. What was so special about this stone that he had to retrieve it, when there were a dozen others equally large that would serve his purpose?

He emerged from the bushes, the front of his raincoat ripped, chalky mud on his hands. He held the stone under one arm. He was at a disadvantage down there, I thought; the embankment was steeper and less easy to climb on that side: when he neared the top I could push him back, no problem. I tried to make up my mind whether to do this or not, as he puffed and panted, clutching tussocks of grass and unsafe twigs. Or I could pick up handfuls of grit from the railway line and pelt him with them. But I did neither.

"Oi, give us some help, can't you?"

I laughed. "I'd be an accessory after the fact," I said.

"What?"

"Nothing."

"Are you being rude? 'Cos if you are . . ." He clenched his free hand in what he presumably felt was a menacing gesture, but down there he merely looked comic and insignificant, and I laughed again. "You'll get a bunch of fives in a minute, mate," he said.

"Oh yes? You and whose army?"

Eventually he succeeded in reaching the top. He replaced the stone on the rail and stood with one foot on it, like someone in those old photographs of pith-helmeted men in the jungle who've just shot a tiger. He appeared much less comic now we were on the same level, more like an escaped lunatic who might turn dangerous at any moment. We stared at each other for some while, then he took his foot off the stone, and walked slowly backwards until he was about as far away from it as I was. I was standing with my hands in my pockets; he squatted on his haunches. You could stick a giant compass in this stone, I thought, and draw a circle; we'd both be on the circumference, on opposite sides.

"You won't get away with it, you know," I said in a loud voice. My mother had spoken like that on one occasion to a butcher who had told her there was no pork in his shop when a large joint of it was very obviously sitting on the counter. But whereas she had sounded most imperious, and the butcher had turned servile and said "Madam may have whatever madam wishes," I did not succeed, I thought, in carrying much conviction. The boy made no reply. "If the train's derailed," I said, trying another tack, "you'll go to prison." No answer. "People might be killed!" Silence. "My cousin's on the train," I finished, but it sounded lame.

He stood up, rummaged around in his pockets, and produced a battered-looking cigarette which he lit with a cheap flashy lighter.

"And that's illegal too," I said.

"What is?" I was startled; I'd almost forgotten that he could talk.

"Smoking at your age."

"Why?"

"You're too young to smoke."

"Who says so?"

"I say so." I was beginning to feel bolder: the invisible circle round the stone was a boundary, and in my own territory I had the illusion of being safe. To enter the circle was breaking into no man's land; chancy, dangerous.

"Never heard anything about smoking being illegal," he said, as if he was taking my remark seriously.

"It is when you're only four years old." He glared at me. "What's your name, anyway?"

"Sid."

"Sid! What kind of a name is that?" I felt that with

everything I uttered I was regressing into some daft childhood ritual.

The train whistled in the distance; it was just crossing the river this side of Itchen Abbas, about a mile away, and I could hear the noise of it starting up the gradient to Alresford, chuffa-chuffa, chuffa-chuffa, chuffa-chuffa. I saw again in my mind's eye the train hitting the stone, the engine leaving the rails, my aunt's grief-frozen face as she heard the news of Nic's death. I walked towards the stone.

So did he. I stopped; he stopped. Another blast from the train's whistle pushed me forward again, and he responded: we were both now less than a yard from the stone. This near he really did look nasty: the face was all vacant except for the eyes which seemed to glower, sullenly, as if he wished, for no conceivable reason, to hit out and inflict pain. The stone had to be removed from the line, but there did not seem to be any way I could possibly do it. I couldn't kick it off; it was so heavy I would only stub my toes. If I dived down to snatch it he would overpower me at once. Should I turn and run towards the train, waving my arms frantically? Fine, if Mr Bowles happened to see me, but if he did not I would be killed, and I knew, from the time I had been in the cab of the engine, that he did not spend every second looking out of the window ahead. He might be chatting to Nic during those crucial moments, and I would be wiped off the face of the earth.

The train was nearer; the chuffa-chuffa became a metallic clang-clanging of wheel, piston and track. At the far end of the cutting the dark shape of the engine loomed, white smoke streaming out like a subterranean cloud. Still I dithered. The engine was leaping in size, a huge black monster, and its noise was terrifying. The train derailed, or me beaten up by this crazy boy; those were the alternatives. Put like that, the choice seemed simple. I rushed for the stone, experiencing the sensation I always felt jumping off the high diving-board in the swimming pool: horrifying, but it can't last for ever. I threw myself away from the engine, clutching the stone in best rugby fashion, and at the same moment the boy landed on me. The train trundled past, the ground trembling under its weight, the screech and roar of it more frightening than its size or nearness, like a giant in agony. I caught a fleeting glimpse of Nic waving from the cab as I and the boy tripped over the edge of the embankment and fell, out of control, skin and clothes tearing and wrenching on thorn and bramble.

When we came to a standstill I found myself lying on top of him, my hands holding the stone just above his face. There was fear in his eyes. No, of course I would not: but let him sweat for a second or two. We were both winded, both bleeding, but there was no real damage. I threw the stone away.

I didn't know how to use my advantage; alarm at what he might do if I struck the first blow stopped me. The hesitation was fatal. He pushed me off with one heave, and before I could stand up he had grabbed hold of my hair and jerked my head back so fiercely that the embankment turned vertical and I was staring into his eyes. I had no time to do anything such as shift my legs to kick him: he swung his clenched fist into my face; light exploded and the willows by the stream shot sideways into view, in double vision, as my left eyeball seemed to be squeezed into my skull. A second blow, wet and slippery on the mouth, and my teeth scrunched together somewhere in the top of my head. Then he was gone.

I staggered to my feet and shouted every four-letter word I could think of. The train drowned some of them with the squeal of its coaches as the brakes were applied, with the long hissing sigh of satisfaction as it halted in the station, and the slam of doors. For a moment or two, before it gathered up its strength and the loud snorts from the engine indicated that it was on its way to Ropley, there was silence, and those expletives rang out over the countryside for anyone who was nearby to listen to and be shocked. But the boy was already too far off to hear them, a dark raincoated figure fleeing along the row of poplar trees.

I sat down. There was pain in one eye and in my nose, and my teeth jarred. I touched my mouth. Blood. The train, entering the cutting, snuffled and babbled away to itself, growing gradually quieter, the white ribbon in the fields marking its progress. The smoke thinned, disappeared; the noise was a distant whisper, then nothing. And I became aware of gentle soothing sounds, the wind in the grass, the murmur of the stream, the call of a moorhen. Despite the ache in my head and the throbbing in my lips, I didn't feel I had been beaten: I had pulled the stone from the rail, defeated his crazy intentions. A black speck which might have been a crow, but which I knew was a raincoat, appeared in the field above the fulling mill, running for the horizon, and soon after that it vanished in the trees.

I heard feet treading the grit on the line above me. They slowed and stopped. "So there you are," Nic said as he scrambled down to join me. "My God! What a mess you look!" He plucked a blade of grass to chew. "What were you doing fighting on the railway line? You could easily have been *killed*! Mr Bowles was looking out of the *other* window, and his eyesight isn't too brilliant anyhow. Who was it?"

"I don't know. He said his name was Sid."

"Sid who?"

"I don't know!"

"There's no-one called Sid in Alresford. Probably made it up." I remembered my invention, Maurice Bartlett. "What was it all about?"

I told him. I felt pleased that I'd saved his life, many people's lives perhaps. But Nic didn't look immensely grateful. His only comment was that my swearing could be heard from the station platform, and Colonel Ramsbottom, who was coming home early from work, had said, "Tut-tut!"

"Compared with a wrecked train," I said, "it doesn't seem very important."

"Pooh! The train would have stayed on the track anyway! You needn't have bothered yourself about the stone; the weight of the engine would have smashed it to smithereens." This remark shocked me rigid. If it was true, then all my efforts had been worthless. Torn clothes, bleeding, pain, screwing up courage in the first place, the certainty of trouble when I returned home: all for nothing.

"Are you sure the weight of the engine would crush it?" I asked.

"Yes. Pow! Just like that!"

I sat at the bottom of the embankment for a while, shoulders hunched, gloom shrouding me like a fog. Nic prattled on about the train journey; he'd been inside the signal box at Winchester, extremely interesting . . .

I stood up and walked off. "See you later," I said.

"Here! What's the matter with you today?"

I didn't answer. I walked back to the house, hoping to get indoors before Mum and Aunt Bridie arrived home from their shopping expedition. If I could clean myself up a bit and change my clothes, I might escape the inevitable lecture, but my luck was certainly out: I ran into them at the front gate, and there was an instant duet of demands to know what in Heaven's name I had been doing. "Just look at yourself!" they chorused, several times. As if I could: there were no mirrors growing on the trees in our garden. I was hustled inside and sent to the bathroom. My mother didn't leave me alone for a single moment; she followed me everywhere and poured a raging torrent of words over me. Disgrace, savagery, hooliganism, figured very prominently, as did phrases like "not worth buying you decent clothes", "can't understand what gets into you", and "end up in a remand home!" I said yes and no in what I hoped were the correct places, and told her as little as possible of the incident.

At tea-time, when she had calmed down, I asked her what would happen if you put a large stone on a railway track; would it wreck a train?

"Michael, if that's what you're thinking of doing next, you certainly *will* end up in a remand home! I don't know what you—"

"No, no!" I said. "I just wondered, that's all."

"Of course it would wreck a train! It's happened before now. Always some vandal—"

"The weight of the train would crush it," said Nic, his cheeks bulging with bread and raspberry jam.

"Don't interrupt when Nora's talking," Aunt Bridie said. "And don't speak with your mouth full."

I appealed to my aunt: "Which of them is right?"

"Your mother, of course. There was a train crash a few years ago caused in exactly that way. Can't remember where it was, some place up north I think. And people were killed. I do remember that."

"Why do you want to know?" my mother asked.

I was silent. "Because he was fighting with some idiot who put a stone on the line," Nic told them.

The two adults immediately wanted to hear all the details, and I didn't feel like telling them, for some reason I couldn't fathom out. But I had to. "I think you deserve a medal," was my mother's verdict. "I'm sorry I went on at you earlier. I didn't realize."

"That boy should be reported to the police!" Aunt Bridie said, bristling with drama and indignation. Alresford hadn't experienced such excitement for years, evidently. "What's his name?"

"Sid."

"Sid what?"

"I don't know."

"It's a false name," Nic informed her. "An alias. But don't worry. We'll find out who he really is."

"You do so," said my aunt, "and I shall tell the police. People like that need to be taught a lesson!"

"I'd like to tie him up to the railway line," I said. "Just as they did on old silent films. Only he wouldn't get away at the last moment."

"That's not very nice," Aunt Bridie said, with a shiver. "Eye for an eye. That's not right."

"It's what I feel."

After tea I went out. I had no aim in mind, no place I particularly wanted to go to, but it was a warm and pleasant evening, better than being indoors. It looked as if there would be a fine sunset; the orange light shimmered and danced on the stream. Columns of gnats hovered over the water and a fish occasionally broke the surface. I found myself by the fulling mill, staring at the water-butt and the thatch, the gap between them, then shook my head: it was impossible. Not, it suddenly dawned on me, if I could find something, wood perhaps, several pieces of wood, and pile them on top of the water-butt. I hunted round, but there was nothing suitable. Eventually, in a thicket of trees some distance away, I discovered exactly what I needed—an old wooden wheel that had once belonged to a cart. It was not rotten, so it would take my weight, but it was extremely heavy. However, I managed, and, gasping for breath, I had the thing in place at last. From then on it was simple. I stood on the rim of the wheel and heaved myself up by placing my elbows on the top of the exposed wall; soon I was peering down the chimney. It was an easy jump to the hearth, no great height, particularly if I lowered myself gently, fingers holding on to the chimney pot, then let go. Two considerations stopped me: another set of clothes would undoubtedly be ruined and I couldn't see whether it was possible to climb up again. But, well, there is no time like the present; another opportunity might not occur. I jumped.

When my eyes became used to the gloom I began to realize that a few years ago I'd have thought what a superb place this was, a perfect headquarters, for any sort of activity kids might want a hide-out for. This had obviously been the living room of the mill. You could light a fire in the hearth; there was even a built-in cupboard where food could be stored. Nic would want to camp here, if Aunt Bridie would let him. It was summer; the nights weren't cold, and he had a sleeping-bag. I didn't see why on earth she should object.

A noise from the roof made me leap out of my skin. Someone else was climbing down the chimney! I hid in the furthest corner of the room. Crash! He landed in the hearth, a great black shadow, crouching. He straightened up. I wasn't one hundred per cent certain because of the darkness, but . . . yes, it was! No doubt of it: the boy who had put the stone on the rail. He seemed to know the place, or, at any rate, he didn't bother to look round as I had done. He went over to a door, opened it, and disappeared into the room beyond. Immediately the roaring of the water underneath the mill ceased; where he was must be directly over the stream.

My first instinct was to turn and run, scramble up the chimney and get away as quickly as I could. But . . . why should I? I had as much right to be there as he did (i.e. none at all). I owed him a few nasty blows on the face, and I had the advantage of surprise. What was he doing? I never found out. Just staring at the rushing water, perhaps. I stood behind the door, waiting. Then, above the noise of the stream, I heard his footsteps. And I jumped on him with a blood-curdling yell.

It wasn't a fight: it didn't even last long enough to be called a scrap. He cowered away, whimpering, then sprang for the chimney. He was up it and gone in a matter of seconds. I don't think he had any idea of who I was; maybe he thought I was a wild animal, a ghost even. There was no doubt, however, that he was terrified out of his wits.

Some while later I followed him up the chimney. It was not a difficult climb, plenty of toe-holds, but it was very sooty. My hands were black, and probably my face was too. My mother would be cross, but not so much as before, because at least I hadn't torn my clothes. Anyway, I couldn't be bothered to worry about what she would have to say; I was trying to sort out a mass of complicated feelings. I'd stopped the train being derailed. I'd found Nic the most splendid hide-out ever. I was quits with that boy. But it was all . . . a part of me I wanted to get away from. Everything about life at Alresford was fine if you were a child, but not if you were sixteen. Nothing happened in this place to help you put away childish things.

2. The Lambeth Walk

My mother and my aunt were both musical, a gift I did not inherit, much to my mother's sorrow. I like classical music, but I can't play an instrument or sing a note that's even mildly pleasant to hear. When Nic had gone to bed, Aunt Bridie would sometimes play the piano and Mum would sing, old Irish ballads mostly, songs of death and exile and lovers' hearts' broken and people getting themselves a-hanged for a-wearing of the green. These performances usually drove me up to my room, or out of the house. They rarely disturbed Nic's sleep however, unless the two women were drinking Guinness at the time, but on the night I returned from climbing into the fulling mill he was woken by a tremendous clatter from downstairs. It was not the piano on this occasion, but the record player at ninety million decibels, accompanied by a great deal of mysterious bumping noises and cries of "Nora, you're doing it all wrong!" and "You've forgotten it, Bridie! Though you never knew how to do it in the first place, did you?"

I was in the bathroom carefully examining the reflection of my body in the mirror, and wondering what girls would think of it, and would I always be as thin as a beanpole. I put my underwear back on and opened the door; Nic was kneeling on the carpet at the top of the stairs, peering through the banisters. "They're dancing," he said.

"They're *what*?"

"Dancing. Ssh."

The record player was telling anyone who cared to

listen how to do the Lambeth Walk:—

Any time you're Lambeth way,
Any evening, any day,
You'll find us all—doing the Lambeth Walk.
Every little Lambeth gal
With her little Lambeth pal,
You'll find 'em all—doing the Lambeth Walk. Oi!

My mother and my aunt emerged from the sitting room, arms round each other, kicking their legs in the air. Mum was waving a bottle of Guinness with her free hand, and Aunt Bridie was singing her head off. They cavorted down the hall and back into the sitting room. "*Doing the Lambeth walk. Oi!*"

"That escaped lunatic Sid kept saying oi," I told Nic. "Oi, you!"

"So you said at tea-time. Maybe that reminded them of this record."

"Have they drunk a lot?"

"I don't know."

The chorus of the song came again, and the two women pranced along the hall once more, their leg kicks even higher. "*OIIII!!*" The record finished, and they broke apart, shouting with laughter.

"Well, it was before our day," Aunt Bridie said eventually. "Momma's favourite piece."

"Yes," my mother answered. "I remember her trying to teach us the steps."

"Let's have another drink."

At the sitting room door Mum saw me staring down from the top of the stairs. "What are you doing?" she demanded.

"You were making one hell of a noise! You woke Nic up!"

The phone rang. Mum—the call was for her—talked for a long time, very quietly and seriously. We couldn't hear a word and Nic, bored, went back to bed; but I was intrigued and stayed on the landing, trying to eavesdrop. She wasn't in the habit of holding lengthy, half-whispered phone conversations.

Some time later she rang off, then said, loudly, "Michael, are you still there? Michael?"

"Yes," I answered.

"Come down. I've something to tell you."

In the sitting room Aunt Bridie was half-way through another bottle of Guinness. Mum said "That was your father," and she stared at the ceiling, a variety of strange expressions flitting across her face. Her hands more than anything else betrayed her agitation. Her right hand was pulling almost savagely at each finger, in turn, of her left hand; I could hear the joints crack. "He wants you to go and stay with him. For a couple of weeks." I was dumbfounded. "I agreed that you should," she said.

"Why?" My voice was high and strangled.

"Because . . . you're old enough, perhaps, to understand."

"Understand what?"

"Is this really a good idea, Nora?" my aunt asked.

Mum looked at her helplessly for a moment, then said "I can't explain. I mean I can't bring myself to explain."

"But you have to!"

"Oh, keep out of it!" my mother said, angrily. Aunt Bridie got up and left the room. "Michael . . . no." She shook her head. "I guess you'll find out when you're there." She added, after a moment, "Your father has . . . some good points. He can be kind, gentle, thoughtful. Well . . . he was. I don't know what he's like now."

"Nobody's asked me if I want to go. I suppose I have a choice?"

"I think you should see him."

"Why?"

"Because he's your father."

"That's no reason to force anyone to do anything."

She sighed, took a sip from the Guinness her sister had left on the table, and said "You shouldn't walk about the house in your underwear. It's not decent."

"I don't want to go!"

She then said one word which astonished me: astonished me because I don't remember her ever saying it to me before, at least not in that tone of voice. The word was "Please".

Which was why I found myself two days later bound for a suburb of Bournemouth with the very odd name of Pokesdown. Normally I would have enjoyed the journey, changing trains at Winchester, and seeing the complex railway junctions at Eastleigh and Southampton—one of my mother's favourite stories about her childhood in the second world war was of being marooned in a crowded train at Eastleigh for nine hours while German bombs deluged on Southampton and smashed the place to bits. I'd often been to Eastleigh and Southampton, but always by car or bus; I wanted to know if their stations were anything like the mental pictures I'd obtained from my mother's reminiscences. There would certainly be some worthwhile railway paraphernalia to observe in Southampton, where I had to change trains yet again. And stations en route with names that interested me, like Totton and Sway. And Pokesdown, of course.

But I could't concentrate on any of this. I was too worried about meeting my father. No amount of pestering my mother—and Aunt Bridie when Mum was out of the house—had given me any explanation of why he had left his wife and young son to go and live in Bournemouth. There had subsequently been a divorce, but I knew that, just as I knew what my father looked like in photographs of thirteen years ago; and that he was a writer of children's books, that he hadn't remarried and didn't have a girlfriend. (On this last point Mum was always curiously certain, even though they had not been in touch with one another for more than a decade.) After the Lambeth Walk evening both women went round the house grim-faced and tight-lipped, scarcely speaking; so it was Nic who supplied me with one detail I had not heard before. "He owns a house on the cliffs in Boscombe," he said, "and he shares it with the harp player of the Wessex Phil-harmonic Symphony Orchestra."

"How do you know that?"

"Mum told me. Ages ago."

"Why didn't you tell *me*?"

"Didn't think it worth mentioning. Anyway . . . I suppose I thought you knew."

"But . . . he doesn't have another wife. Or a girlfriend."

"The harpist is a he."

Perhaps my dad is queer, I thought, then laughed at such a silly notion even entering my head. What did I really think of him? When I was seven, eight, nine, I used to feel angry that he wasn't around. Sometimes *very* angry. A whole bit of life that was mine by right was being denied me. It was hurtful to see other kids with their fathers playing football, swimming, or even just walking along a road. They had a dad and I did not. I felt jealous and wounded. Mum did little to assuage these emotions, indeed possibly aided and abetted them, though whether consciously or not I don't know. In the rare moments when the subject of my father came up in conversation, she would always run him down; he was unreliable, or self-centred, or didn't understand other people. She never suggested he was some kind of monster, just a rather faulty man who hadn't grown up properly. But, I would say to myself, he invariably sends us money, every month, dead on time.

Sometimes I was teased at school for having only one parent, but I usually settled that by punching the offending kid on the nose, quite hard. When I reached the age of eleven and went to school in Winchester, I was no longer angry and sad. I'd become used to the facts of existence, and was indifferent about my father: he didn't live with us; there was nothing I or anyone else could do to remedy that, and there were plenty of other things to worry about or enjoy. Until the Lambeth Walk evening. As the train rumbled on through Totton and Sway, I began to shiver inside, like a leaf in autumn. If only she hadn't said "Please!" By the time I arrived at Pokesdown, Alresford and that afternoon I'd yanked the stone off the railway line seemed light years off in the past.

He hadn't aged a great deal, to judge from the photographs I'd seen, though his hair was greyer than I'd imagined. He was wearing a tee-shirt and shorts, which rather surprised me, and he looked suntanned and fit. He was nervously smoking a cigarette. I recognized him at once: he didn't recognize me, but I told myself not to be upset by that; how could he possibly know who I was? I was three when he saw me last, and now we were the same height.

"Dad . . .?"

"Mike? Is it you, Mike?"

"Yes."

He smiled and laughed, then shaking his head, exclaimed "Terrible! I could have walked by you in the street and not have known!" We stared at each other for a while in silence; almost, I guess, as if we were drinking in each other's appearance, fixing it in our minds like a snap-shot. Then he said, "The car's outside. Let's get back to the house."

During the drive he asked how my mother was and Aunt Bridie and Nic, and wondered how I'd amuse myself in Bournemouth for two weeks—as if, I thought, this visit had been thrust on him unwillingly instead of occurring at his own request—and he wanted to know what foods I did not like eating. He hoped I'd get on well with Adrian, the harpist, who was the cook of the household; "I've never learned to do that sort of thing," he said, laughing again. The beaches were superb at this time of the year, he told me; I could, if I wanted to, swim every day. He was going to a concert that night. The Wessex Philharmonic Symphony were playing at the Winter Gardens, and maybe I'd like to come too; he usually went to all their concerts as Adrian provided free tickets. "It's Mahler's tenth symphony," he said. "Do you know it?"

"No."

"It's a bit . . . esoteric."

"What's that mean?"

"Out of the ordinary. Do you like classical music?"

"Some. Yes."

"Good. That's settled then."

What was settled? Nothing, as far as I could see. Maybe this visit *had* been imposed on him; could Mum . . . could Mum have deliberately arranged it? If so, why? And as far as classical music was concerned, I knew what I liked: Tchaikovsky, Beethoven, Mozart. The little Mahler I'd heard was a confusing jumble of sounds, too much going on at once.

There were no buildings on the other side of Boscombe Overcliff Drive, so from my bedroom window there was a marvellous view: grass that abruptly stopped on the edge of the cliffs, and beyond that a great expanse of blue sea dancing and winking in the summer sunshine. The beach was out of sight, tucked under the cliffs, but in two minutes I could be running through warm sand into the waves. The whole sweep of Poole Bay was visible, from Swanage and Studland on the right to the two piers, and on the left the dunes and beaches that led up to the great lump of land called Hengistbury Head. Out in the sea were the jagged rocks and lighthouse of the Needles, the nearest corner of the Isle of Wight, its feet and toes.

Perhaps I could enjoy myself here. Bournemouth seemed large, and inviting—it couldn't be worse, for a teenage kid in the summer, than Alresford. Dad didn't want me around all the time, I assumed—he was probably working on a book and would need peace and quiet. Adrian, who wasn't at home when we arrived, would probably be out most days practising his harp.

I liked Boscombe Overcliff Drive. The name was a help to start with—it sounded so unusual. And rather grand. "Oh, I live in Boscombe Overcliff Drive" had a better ring to it than Grange Road, Alresford. During my first hours alone that afternoon I explored the immediate neighbourhood; the houses, all built before the second world war, were solid, reassuring structures that didn't look as if they'd blow away in the first gales of autumn, like windy Tralee. They had big, established gardens, lovingly tended by their owners who seemed to be frail old men and women in their seventies and eighties. "Bournemouth is costa geriatrica," my father said when I asked where the kids were. "An old people's haven. They come here to rot and die. I think Adrian and I are the youngest people in the whole road."

"There must be *some* kids around."

"Oh, you'll find plenty on the beach," he said.

He was right. At the foot of the cliffs, just below where he lived, was another world—families, young lovers, and kids playing games and swimming and snoozing in the sun. The sea was warm, too: I really enjoyed swimming on that beach. Back on the cliff top was the grass, the old ladies huddling in shelters and looking at the sea or walking their dogs; an immense profusion of pine trees with their gummy, resiny scents drifting on the wind; the summer gardens—roses, vivid scarlet geraniums, flashy zinnias, montbretia a dazzling orange, and cool blue scabious. At a turn in the road was the building that dominated the area—a block of flats, but no ordinary block of flats: it was like a huge Moorish palace all curlicues, turrets, pergolas and zig-zag ornamentation as if an Arab sheikh had installed himself there with room enough for a harem of a thousand wives. "A millionaire's folly," Dad said. "I don't know when it was built; turn of the century, I guess. Been split up into flats for years now, and it costs the absolute earth to live there." It gave the right touch of the bizarre and the mysterious to what I already felt was a totally different place from sleepy old Alresford and dull old Winchester, even though I was only fifty miles away and still in the same county. Bournemouth was as foreign as if I'd been whisked off to the coast of Morocco.

Dad's house was also something different, quite unlike shabby Tralee which was too much lived in and not always clean, its garden neglected as Mum and Aunt Bridie said there was never a spare moment to weed flower-beds and prune shrubs. Nic and I were the only members of our family who did any work out of doors, and that was confined to mowing the lawn in order to earn our allowances. Dad was enthusiastic about his well-kept garden, particularly the begonias in the greenhouse, and the pond with its goldfish and red water-lilies. "But it does take up an enormous amount of time," he said, "especially when you have to do it yourself."

"Doesn't Adrian give you a hand?" I asked.

"All Adrian ever does out here is to demand that half the plants get moved around. He has a mania for wanting to dig things up and shove them in somewhere else."

"Does he actually do that?"

"I won't let him."

The living room and the kitchen were as neat as the garden, and I said Tralee was never like this. I expected Dad to pick up the cue and ask me why, or make some comment about Mum not caring enough, but his mind was more preoccupied with his own house. "I sometimes think this place is too much of a museum," he said. "I prefer my home to look as if people live in it. At least in my study I can enjoy making a mess."

"Why not down here?"

"Adrian tidies everything away. He's extremely house-proud." Adrian wasn't getting a very good press, I thought, and wondered, if that was the case, why Dad decided to share his existence with someone he didn't seem to get on with tremendously well.

"Where is Adrian?" I asked.

"At the Winter Gardens rehearsing the Mahler. It's a very difficult piece, and the harp has quite a lot to do. He's nervous and excited about it: they've never played it before."

He took me upstairs and showed me his study, which was next to my bedroom and had the same view of the sea. On his desk, which was by the window, was a typewriter and a manuscript written in long-hand; if he was lost for inspiration, I supposed, he could look up and enjoy what the weather was doing with the English Channel. The walls were covered with pictures and shelves—there were books, papers, ornaments, and potted plants on every available surface. I noticed a framed photograph of me as a baby. Two shelves were devoted entirely to his own works. "I didn't know you'd written so many," I said.

"Twenty-two published. More than that written; I still get rejections, but I'm hardened to that." I was, I

28

said to myself, the first rejection to which he became hardened.

"There's a lot more than twenty-two here."

"Ah, well, American editions, paperbacks and translations. *The Acacia Tree* was even translated into Afrikaans; Heaven knows why the Dutch South Africans were interested in a second world war story about three English boys in Kent!" He pulled out a book, glanced at it, and replaced it.

"Do you earn a lot of money?"

"Just about enough to keep going."

"Are you famous?"

He laughed. "What a strange question! Does it mean you haven't read any of them?"

"I read them once. It was in the school library." He frowned, as if he was hoping I'd read them all and could give a scholarly dissertation on the subject. Or maybe he'd thought that by reading his books I'd have discovered a way of keeping in touch with him. "The person you learn most about when you read a novel," my English teacher once said, "is the author. He leaves a smudge of himself on every page." But Mum never encouraged me to read Dad's collected masterpieces. Not that she actively discouraged me either; I just felt that she would have been hurt if she'd found me with my nose stuck in the pages of *The Nightmare of Malta* or *The Acacia Tree*. Anyway, as I said, after the age of eleven, I hardly ever thought about Dad at all.

"Which book was it you read?" he asked.

"*The Nightmare of Malta.*"

"Ah. Did you enjoy it?"

"Yes. Yes." I knew I sounded insincere, but I couldn't help that; it was so long ago that I really didn't remember much about it.

"Well, they're all here," he said, waving an arm at the bookshelves. "If you're in the mood, you can read some of them during your stay. But—" he added, a little anxiously, "—don't think you *have* to."

"I will. I'd like to. But . . . what age are they for?"

He winced, as if that was a disagreeable question. "All ages. A novel is a novel is a novel, whether the main character or the reader you have in mind is seven or seventy. But . . . to be more specific . . . I've written children's books, and *young* children's books like *Disappointed Dragons*, and young adult books."

"Young adult? Does that mean for teenagers?"

"Yes."

"I'll try one of those."

Perhaps he didn't care for the way this conversation had developed, for he said "Let's go downstairs now." On the landing he stopped, opened a door, and said "This is Adrian's study." It was a smaller room than Dad's, very uncluttered—a desk that had nothing on it, two chairs, a tiny bookcase, and one picture, a strident violent painting in clashing yellows, reds and purples that showed two cockerels fighting. Their claws and beaks looked murderous, and feathers were flying all over the place. I disliked it at once—it was far too disturbing. It reminded me of my fight with the boy who had put the stone on the railway track.

"I don't think much of it, either," my father said, as if he was reading my thoughts.

But there was one object that was fascinating: certainly not something you'd find in other houses in Boscombe Overcliff Drive, or indeed anywhere else in Bournemouth. Right in the middle of the carpet, so you had to walk round it to get to the corners of the room, was a full-size orchestral harp.

"That is beautiful," I said.

"He plays it like an angel." I plucked it—a gorgeous, resonant low note—then brushed my finger-nails across the top strings, producing a delicious cascade of cacophonous noises like a jet of water in sound. "Don't do that!" Dad said.

"Why not?"

"He goes berserk if anybody touches it."

"Why?"

"I don't know. Something to do with the tuning, I guess." What on earth difference could it possibly make to the tuning, I asked myself, just plucking a few strings? This Adrian seemed to be unpleasant and bad-tempered; I was not much looking forward to meeting him. "We'll go downstairs and have a drink," Dad said. "Then I must put my not so powerful intellect to the job of rustling up something to eat." He laughed. "One of those rare occasions I have to; Adrian has no time between the rehearsal and the performance to come home."

I felt rather relieved at this piece of news. "Am I supposed to wear a tie and a jacket for the concert?"

"No, no. Whatever you want. Do you like omelettes?"

"Yes."

"Omelettes are about the limit of my abilities."

He evidently didn't feel happy in the kitchen with me hovering about while he melted butter in the frying pan, cracked eggs into a bowl, and put asparagus tips (one of my favourites) in a saucepan, so I took my beer into the garden and sat by the pond, staring at the goldfish. What a strange day it was; but it could not, whatever the particular circumstances of Dad's life might have been, have turned out other than strange. I liked him, I was surprised to discover; I could even be fond of him. As with any son to his father? Perhaps not that, exactly. Was the hurt and rejection and anger of my childhood still simmering away, ready to spew out like some volcano deciding to erupt? Probably not, but I couldn't be certain. Some answers to some obvious questions would help, such as why he'd invited me, why now, and why did Mum agree to it; and some answers to questions I didn't know how to put—why did the marriage break down, why did it result in no communication at all for so long, and why did he live with a rather neurotic man he didn't seem to get on with very well? I wanted to say, too, how is it possible to have a son and not think about him for thirteen years? But he'd already answered that, in part, without my having to inquire: the kids, he said, who were the main characters in his books, when they weren't himself as a boy, were me.

"How is that?" I asked. "You don't know me. You didn't even know what I looked like till today."

"True." He smiled. "So I had to make it all up."

"Then they aren't me."

"They're what I hoped you were. Hope you are. Sometimes what I feared might happen to you."

I had a sneaking suspicion for a moment that the me of the books might be of more interest to him than the real me; that perhaps the marriage ended because Mum decided she and I were less important to him than his writing. There was no easy way of solving that one; however, time would tell—even if none of the questions was put and none of the answers given, this fortnight would give me something of that smudge my English teacher had talked about. And I could read all the novels, or as many as I could get through.

But why bother? I was already hooked, I suppose. As I said, I liked him. He was so different from Mum. There was something dull and predictable about life at Tralee; the two women dancing the Lambeth Walk was the limit of the unusual. Here, anything might happen.

"Dinner's ready," Dad called. A cheese and mushroom omelette, chips and asparagus. "I'm afraid it's nothing special," he said, "but I hope it's O.K."

It was fine, and I said so, which pleased him. There is a vulnerable side to my father, I thought; he needs to be protected. I don't know why this idea should have entered my head—there was no reason I could fathom for such an intuition. Protection from what? Or whom?

The concert hall, I learned from the notes in my programme, was called the Winter Gardens because in Victorian times that was exactly what it had been—a huge glass-house containing all sorts of exotic plants that could not be grown out of doors in the winter. People paid money to come in and look at the flowers, drink tea and listen to a little café orchestra playing music in the background. It was not a commercial success, however, and when it went bankrupt the Wessex Philharmonic Symphony bought it, replaced all the glass with brick, and turned it into a proper concert hall. The effect was somewhat hideous—the Winter Gardens looked like an ancient and dilapidated cinema.

I had never been to a symphony concert before. There was hardly much opportunity for that sort of thing in Alresford, and, besides, Mum and my aunt would rather perform their Irish ballads than listen to Beethoven. Dad looked surprised when I told him that, for me, this evening was a first experience; "In that case, Mahler's tenth is going to be a baptism of fire," he said.

"What do you mean?"

"It's very long and some of it's very slow."

There were only two works on the programme, the overture to Mozart's *The Magic Flute*, then the symphony. There was no interval. "How long?" I asked.

"An hour and a quarter, maybe an hour and a half."

"I know the overture. It takes less than ten minutes."

"It's just something to warm us up."

I didn't really need to be warmed up; it was a hot evening and the Winter Gardens was stuffy and airless. I sat back and prepared myself for acute boredom. The orchestra tuning their instruments, however, was quite interesting, despite the horrible noise they made. I didn't even know the names of some of the objects they were blowing and scraping. "What's that?" I asked. "And that? And that?"

"A double bassoon," Dad said, smiling. "A celesta— a bit like a tiny piano. What else? Oh, that's a bass clarinet."

Adrian was one of the last players to arrive. He went quickly to his seat, pulled the harp towards himself till it rested on his shoulder, then plucked a few strings and made a shower of notes down the scale, not unlike the jet of water I'd created on the harp in his study, though rather more harmonious than my effort. He seemed satisfied with the sound, for he stopped, pushed the harp into an upright position, and turned his head to survey the audience. We were in the fourth row, and he was obviously looking for us, for when he saw Dad he winked. Dad smiled back and nodded his head slightly. Adrian then returned to the serious business of twanging the harp, making sure it was properly in key I suppose, and ignored us for the rest of the evening.

I'd expected a man of Dad's age—forty-five—but Adrian appeared to be much younger; and Dad confirmed this when I asked. "He'll be twenty-six next month," he said. I found this oddly disconcerting; I don't know why. I had assumed people's friends were usually as old as they were themselves. Mine were, give or take a year or two, and nearly all Mum's and Aunt Bridie's friends and acquaintances were middle-aged housewives with kids at school. It gave them something to talk about, I imagined. "Nic does this or Michael said that," were standard topics of conversation my mother and my aunt had with Mrs Eggins next door or Mrs Williams and Mrs Blenkinsop down the road, who usually replied with "Susan's doing so-and-so and Chris has just been to such-and-such." Bor-*ing*! But what on earth did a man of twenty-six and a man of forty-five, who shared a house together, find to talk about?

Long, curly, almost golden hair; tall and handsome. His face—he wasn't close to us of course, but not so far away that I couldn't make out some of the details—was triangular, with high cheek-bones. He was fit and bronzed, like Dad. I couldn't see his eyes clearly; they were hidden under a forehead that seemed to jut out too far. I didn't like that. But, I thought, if he was my age, he'd be the sort of kid boys at school envied or loathed, because *all* the girls would go bananas about him.

"Does he have a girlfriend?" I asked, as the applause for the conductor died down.

Dad looked puzzled. "No," he said. "Didn't Nora . . . ? Ssssh! The music's about to begin."

The orchestra launched into the busy, bubbling overture to *The Magic Flute*, which finished all too soon, I thought. I enjoyed it. It didn't require a harp at any point; Adrian sat with his arms folded throughout, a somewhat severe expression on his face.

More applause. "Now for Symphony Number Ten in F Sharp Major," Dad said. "I'm looking forward to this. Never heard a live performance of it. It's a most unusual key, F sharp. Very difficult."

"Ssssh," I said.

3. Fights and friendships

I certainly wasn't bored: my reactions were more positive. I hated it. Almost every moment from beginning to end, I *hated* it! It stank of death and yearning for death. I don't know if music can be about things you can define like that, indeed if it can be about anything at all, but that's what it said to me. There were parts of it with tunes that were beautiful and excruciating at the same time, like a man looking at a glorious sunset which was always fading, or gazing at a vision of something for ever beyond his ability to possess—the harp had a lot of work to do here; as the violins soared slowly and inexorably upwards, singing of dying and joys lost in the past, it provided a kind of anchor to the song floating far above. I kept thinking of someone in bed, towards the end of a fatal illness, constantly recalling the happy days that are no more. At other moments the music was like stabs of pain, as if the composer were lacerating himself with a knife and masochistically enjoying what he was doing; and at one point, after a long, slow, very quiet passage that faded away to nothing at all, there came a noise from the orchestra so loud that I almost jumped out of my seat—a succession of chords so violent and harsh that I had a mental picture of a cathedral organ gone crazy, creating sounds that disintegrated the architecture into a sea of stone and dust.

My father said very little as we left the Winter Gardens, and I was glad; it was difficult enough to adjust, after that, to normal life outside—people talking and laughing as they came out of pubs; cars and buses changing gear; a wind off the sea whispering in the pines—let alone have a sensible discussion about music. But in the car, on the way home, he said "I suppose you didn't like it."

"No."

"It was torture?"

"Awful. Unbearable. Hideous!"

"Hideous? I used to hate it too, when I first heard it. But it grows on you with time. I . . . let's say . . . admire it. But I don't think I could listen to it every night of the week."

"I never want to hear it again."

Dad laughed. "Adrian loves it; he always has done. He says it's like casting out devils. It makes him feel better."

"He must be a very strange man."

"Well . . . you can make your own mind up about that. But I'm sorry the programme wasn't more suitable . . . It just so happened to be what was on the menu this evening."

"That's O.K. It was an interesting experience."

I felt tired. It had been a day of so many new emotions, impressions and events that, when we reached home, I wanted to go straight to my room and sleep, but Dad said "Hang on a moment; Adrian will be back soon and I think you should meet him. In any case . . . we ought to talk." In the long silence that ensued he poured himself a large gin and tonic and lit a cigarette. "Adrian and I are . . . have . . ."

"I'd guessed that," I answered. Which was more or less true. A curious sensation—my heart sinking, almost literally I thought: I could follow its progress down through my stomach, my left leg and out of my body via the foot and the big toe.

"I asked Nora to tell you, but she obviously didn't. I thought she said she would . . . but our phone conversation was a bit . . . difficult. Mike . . . don't hate me for it."

I looked up from the floor where I'd been watching what I imagined was the progress of my heart across the carpet, and stared him straight in the eye. "I don't hate you at all," I said. My heart was suddenly back where it normally was, though thumping rather more loudly and quickly than usual.

He drank some gin. "That's why the marriage ended. Why I had to leave . . . her. And you."

"For Adrian?"

"No, not for Adrian!" He smiled. "Lord! He would have been only thirteen at the time! For . . . the principle of the thing, I suppose. Look, do you want a drink? After this and Mahler's tenth you deserve one."

"A vodka?" Mum occasionally let me have beer or wine with our Sunday dinner; I'd never tried vodka. "What do you mean," I asked, as he poured it, "the principle of the thing?"

"That . . . I preferred men. That it wasn't a problem your mother and I could talk through and resolve. That it was better for both of us . . . to part. I didn't know anything of this when we got married. Some vague idea, perhaps, but I thought it would go away. Do you understand what I'm talking about?"

"Not really."

He sighed. "You must have heard about homosexuality."

"Of course. I reckon . . . I'm very much looking forward to sex. When I'm ready. With girls." I was surprised at what I'd just said. Not that it wasn't true, but this man, even if he was my father, was until today a complete stranger. One only mentioned things like that to friends at school, not to one's parents! Imagine saying that to Mum! She'd have hysterics.

"Girls," he said, smiling. "In the plural, I see."

Why not? The vodka, I decided, was going to my head. "I've never met a homosexual. We laugh and

38

joke about them at school, but . . ."

"Now you have met one."

"Yes."

"You've had quite a day, Mike."

"You can say that again! Dad . . . you're my *dad*!" I burst into tears, and accidentally knocked my drink over. It dripped down the table and on to the carpet. He jumped to his feet and came towards me, but I ran out of the room, up the stairs, and, throwing off my clothes, I fell into bed.

I woke from a delicious dream about a girl I'd noticed on the beach yesterday. It faded, like the bitter-sweet paragraphs of Mahler's symphony, as I remembered last night's conversation. I had a profound feeling of relief—at any rate, I said to myself, the pleasure I got from the dream proves that homosexuality isn't something you inherit. Nor is it contagious, like a disease. But Dad does *that* with men? With Adrian? Ugh! What could have happened to make him want to? It was like . . . it was like . . . the inexplicable ugliness of that boy. The stone on the railway line. Oh, years and years in the past when I was a child that seemed, not just earlier this week! Alresford, I said, had nothing for teenagers, nothing to help you grow up, but now I wanted to be a child once more, like Nic with his simple delight in trains, a child with questions to ask of adults who would give reassuring answers, not find myself in this . . . this muddle, this turmoil! Yet hadn't I said to Dad—quite truthfully—that there was something about growing up I was looking forward to very much?

I'd go back down to the beach, I decided, and see if the girl I'd dreamed about was there today.

I met Adrian over breakfast. Even though he had been some distance from us last night, the impression I'd got of his appearance was correct. The eyes—piercingly blue—were partly hidden by the low, protruding forehead. It was as if someone were watching you from a cave.

"So what did you think of the Mahler?" he asked.

"I didn't like it."

He turned at once on Dad. "There! What did I tell you, Peter? I said it would be beyond him, didn't I! You should have done something else yesterday evening."

"No need to make a fuss about it!"

"I'm not making a fuss about it!" In fact, he seemed to be angrier with every word he spoke. "I just wish you'd have more sense, that's all."

"Well, all right." Dad was now getting rather cross. "No point in arguing over it."

"You never admit to making a single mistake! It always ends up with 'no point in arguing over it'."

"Why are you trying to provoke a quarrel for no reason at all? I wish you could learn to control yourself a bit better."

I appeared to have been forgotten about. They were glaring at each other as if I wasn't in the room.

"Control myself!" Adrian exclaimed. "What do you mean?"

"You're being insensitive and childish. Why? There happens to be someone else here, Adrian! My son!"

"Oh, your *son*! *Don't* think you can start using him as a weapon against *me*!"

"Excuse me," my father said, and abruptly left the room.

Adrian sighed, then sat down at the table. He helped himself to toast and marmalade, and I went on eating cornflakes. While he ate he read the newspaper. There was no sense of stillness about anything he did. He seemed to suffer from an excess of nervous energy, waggling and twitching his nose, and when his hands weren't occupied he was rubbing at his fingers or picking at his feet. I was surprised to see that his nails were bitten down to the quick; wouldn't a harpist need to use his nails? He brushed his hair back from his forehead several times, and scowled. If *I* lived with him, I said to myself, I'd be a screaming wreck in ten minutes.

"Life with your father isn't exactly a bed of roses," he said. "Still, it won't be for much longer."

I said nothing. I didn't want to speak; this man was so totally repellent. What on earth was the matter with him? He didn't want me around, that was for sure—but why should he be so resentful and jealous? It won't be for much longer . . . I assumed he meant I was only in the house for a fortnight, but it was oddly phrased. For much longer implied that I'd already been here for some time. Was he suggesting, perhaps, that *he* wouldn't be here much longer?

I finished my cornflakes and left. He was still reading the newspaper: he didn't look up or say anything.

My father was typing, so I knocked on the door. "Come in, come in," he said. "There's never any need to knock."

"Can I go down to the beach?" I asked.

"Of course. Any time you want. Just come and go as you please. Are you O.K.?"

"Yes."

"I'm sorry about that . . . over breakfast. Adrian is rather highly strung . . . I daresay the performance last night took it out of him."

"Maybe he doesn't think it's convenient to have me staying with you."

"I'll decide whether it's convenient or not," Dad said, "to have my own son staying in my own house! Not him!" He paused. "Yes," he went on, "it's *my* house, not his, not jointly owned. He doesn't even pay any rent."

"Why not?" It was none of my business, but it

seemed more and more inexplicable with every passing minute that Dad and Adrian were friends, let alone lovers.

"He doesn't earn enough money. But what money he has, he's very generous with."

"Oh."

"What time will you be back? I thought we might go out after lunch. Explore the town . . . drive to Poole or the New Forest. Would you like that?"

"Very much. I won't be more than an hour or two."

Highly strung! Huh! Just plain nasty. I was lying on my towel, sandy and damp after a long swim that I felt was somehow cleansing. Anyway, I felt better. The girl was nowhere to be seen, so I eyed all the other girls instead. And thought about Dad. I was surprised not to feel much anger about why he'd left Mum and me. I couldn't understand his homosexuality, didn't want to understand it, but I'd accepted it without hesitation, because—well, it was a good reason, I thought, for leaving. I couldn't explain it to myself any better than that. I would have felt more upset if he'd run off with another woman. But it didn't account for why he had not bothered to get in touch with me for thirteen years, hadn't sent me a card or a present on my birthdays or at Christmas. Could that be Mum's fault? Maybe she had refused to let him have any contact with us because any reminder would be a wound. A wound to her, but did she ever consider what *I* wanted, what I felt like? Suddenly I began for the first time in my life to feel bitterness against *her*. Dad had always sent the cheques every month; we lacked nothing and Mum did not have to go out to work. She hadn't done so badly.

He, I thought, had done badly. That he should need a man, and a man as dreadful as Adrian, when the world was full of attractive girls, was a total mystery to me.

The girl I'd met yesterday, the one I'd dreamed

about, walked by. She smiled as she passed, and I said "Hallo."

When I got to the house I could hear voices raised in heated argument. I crept in quietly, tip-toed up to my room . . . but left the door open so I could listen.

"Why has it all been done behind my back?" my father demanded. "Why do I have to be presented with a fait accompli? We could have discussed it, found some way of . . . of combining this with our life here."

"We are discussing it," Adrian said.

"Oh, no, Adrian, we are not discussing anything! You just calmly walk in and announce that you've got a job with the Mersey Philharmonic and expect me to be pleased!"

"Aren't you? Last week you said our life together was tawdry."

"I didn't say I wanted to end it! I was just trying to find ways of improving it."

"You're not interested in me. Not really. Any more than you are in Mike. The only thing that concerns you is writing the next book!"

"Because I need the money, damn it! Not just for myself, but for an ex-wife and a son and you. There's very little time I can afford to spend not working."

"Well, you'll have a bit more now," Adrian said, sarcastically. "I'm going and I'm going for good!"

My father's voice went quiet. "Six years, and all for nothing. I don't believe it."

"I didn't want it to turn out like this."

"But you could still have your home here. Why not?" Dad was pleading now. "This can be your base . . . between engagements, for holidays . . ."

"Peter, if I stay I shall lose whatever little shred of identity I have left. You eat people up! You draw them into some . . . some spell . . I can see you doing it with Mike! Oh, yes! He ought to hate you, but he's already doing the hero-worship bit!"

"Rubbish!"

"It isn't rubbish at all!"

"You're jealous," Dad said. "And you timed this on purpose so it would happen when Mike was here, didn't you? Typical of your spiteful, needy, greedy personality!"

"This is irrelevant," Adrian said. "The fact is I'm going; I'm going for good, and I'm going now! Today! I trust you enough to look after my things . . . the harp . . . until I've found somewhere permanent to live. There is really no point in talking any further."

"Adrian, you're a bastard."

"Probably."

"But . . . I love you."

I fled. Forgetting the need to be quiet, I ran down the stairs, and as I left the house I heard my father say "What's that noise?" and Adrian's answer: "Your son, eavesdropping."

The girl, Miranda, was coming out of the sea as I hurried on to the beach. "You told me you were going out for a drive with your father," she said.

"I think it's been cancelled," I replied, curtly.

"Is something wrong?"

"No." She obviously didn't believe that, so I said "He was having an argument."

She spread her towel out and sat down on it. "Well . . . my parents have arguments, too."

"Mine are divorced. Mum lives . . . miles away. This argument was with someone else."

"Oh." There was a short silence, then she said "You can have lunch with us; I expect it would be all right. I've never brought a strange boy back before and asked him to eat with us, but I shouldn't think they'd object— Mum and Dad, I mean."

"I'd better not."

"We're only having a picnic. Over there." She pointed to a group of people some distance away, along the beach. A man in swimming trunks, placidly smoking a pipe; a woman taking food from a basket and arranging it on a travelling rug; two little kids squabbling. "That's my brother Ben," Miranda said, "and my sister Kate. He's seven and she's six."

"Thanks . . . but . . . I'd rather be by myself for a while."

"And get over it?"

"Yes." I looked at her, and said "You're nice."

She seemed embarrassed. "I'll come back after lunch if you're still here," she said, and, wrapping her towel round herself, she walked off to join her family.

I lay there, letting the warm wind brush my skin; it was like being dressed in silk. I picked up handfuls of dry, hot sand and let it trickle through my fingers. Kids ran in and out of the sea. A woman screamed at the first chill touch of a wave. Two men, quite near me, were playing with a football, kicking it backwards and forwards to each other. Were they, I wondered, like Dad? Or did they have girlfriends? There was no way of telling. How did such people find others like themselves? Did any of it really matter?

No, it didn't really matter. In itself. But why did I have the rotten luck to have one of those for a father? I glanced from time to time at Miranda's family up the beach. The two young ones were now quite calm, eating. Dad was drinking something out of a bottle. Miranda and her mother were talking and laughing together. Happy, happy families. I didn't have one. I did, of course—Mum and Nic and Aunt Bridie. But that wasn't the same—just two broken pieces of families. It wasn't fair. Nothing's *ever* fair.

Miranda returned. "I've brought you some food," she said. "Even Ben couldn't manage to swallow everything." She offered me a cheese and tomato sandwich, a chocolate cup-cake, and an apple.

I was hungry. "Thanks," I said, and took a bite out of the sandwich. "Didn't your mother mind?"

"She joked about having to feed the five thousand, and Dad said why didn't you come over and join us?"

"I've got . . . too many problems to work out."

"Oh?"

But I shook my head. Actually, I was bursting to talk to someone, but I felt shy. How could you say to a girl you'd only met a few hours ago—a girl you wanted to impress—listen, my dad's a pouf? When I'd finished eating I said "Let's go for a walk."

"O.K." She glanced at her watch. "Mum said I wasn't to be too long."

We strolled up the sand to Boscombe pier, then on to the Overcliff Drive and sat in a shelter as the old ladies did to look at the view. This is how it should be, I said to myself, two teenage kids discussing teachers and homework, rock groups, sport: ordinary, normal life.

She lived in Boscombe, I was surprised to discover; I'd assumed she was on holiday—though there was no reason at all, I told myself, to think everybody at the sea was a tourist. Her house was two or three roads away from my father's. Her dad worked in a department store in the centre of Bournemouth; it was early closing day and he had the afternoon off, which was why they had come down to the beach.

"You ought to come and say hallo," she said. "Then Mum won't be worried that I've gone off with an axe murderer."

They were pleasant, easy-going people. "Miranda says you're staying with your father for a week or two," Mrs Dean said. "And that you might be a bit lonely. Come round to our house; you certainly won't be lonely there! I sometimes wish I could get away from the noise and the chaos!"

"You thrive on it," her husband said.

"It's not me," said Ben. "I don't make a racket. It's all Miranda's great trampling friends."

"Trampling?" his father questioned.

Ben nodded, gravely. "Trampling," he insisted.

I said I'd better be going home; Mrs Dean repeated her invitation for me to drop in, and Miranda said she'd see me later. I walked up the cliff-path much happier than when I'd come down. If the situation got any worse, I now had somewhere else to go. Miranda was interesting and pretty. I could, of course, return to Alresford if life with Dad became too embarrassing or intolerable, but I didn't want to go back before my time was up. As I said, I already liked my father.

He was sitting, hunched, in a chair. The Mahler was on the stereo, its agony stabbing and slicing the room. "He's gone," Dad said.

"Already?"

His eyes moved slowly round until they were gazing at me. "What do you mean, already?"

"I .. er . . . heard something of . . . what was happening when I came in at lunch-time."

"Gone. Gone. Gone." The words sounded like an old cracked church bell, tolling for a funeral. "You'd better go too," he said.

"Me? Why?"

"I don't think . . . I'm in a proper state to look after you. This isn't a . . . a good scene."

"I don't want to go."

"My turn to ask why."

"I like it here," I said. The lacerations of the music suddenly changed to the beautiful, bitter-sweet tune— the soaring violins, the anchoring harp. The man in bed, terminally ill, seeing all the lost sunsets.

"I had every reason in the world to leave *him*," Dad said. "Not the other way round. He could be violent. Smashed things up. Kicked me with his heavy, wooden clogs, moody, irritable and selfish. Expected to be given everything and give nothing in return. Jealous, possessive—you name it; he had *all* the faults. Even got angry if I spent five minutes talking to someone he didn't approve of. I want, I want always. Never a moment to consider what *I* might want. Many times I was on the point of telling him to leave. But I never did."

"Why not?"

"Because. That's the only thing I can say . . . because." He smoothed his hair back with his right hand, then stood up, crossed the room and poured himself a gin.

"I don't understand it at all," I said.

"How could you possibly? I'm embarrassed and worried . . . plunging you into this . . . this adult situation. It's wrong."

"Can we do without that music?" The sunset was fading, fading, fading.

"If you like." I took the pick-up off the record, and the silence was sweet. "Mahler is full of self-pity, I know," Dad went on. "Which doesn't help anyone very much. Look . . . if you're hungry, do you think you could find something in the kitchen? I'm not up to putting a meal together tonight. Can you manage the stove?"

"I expect so."

"I'm sorry . . . all I'm fit for is getting drunk. I guess I'm a pretty terrible father."

"Not the usual type." I laughed. "You don't really want me to go home, do you?"

"No."

"Dad . . ." I stopped, not sure how to say it. "I used to hate you, for just not being around. When I got over that, I didn't think about you at all. I couldn't have cared less. Now I've met you . . . there's . . . I don't know how to put it . . . we're actually able to talk! I said yesterday I was looking forward to . . . well, sex. How many boys of sixteen are there who don't want that? But how many of them feel they can say so to their fathers? It's odd . . . something weird's happened. Last week I was a child playing games on the railway line with Nic. Now . . . "

"Ah." He stared at his drink. "In standing water between boy and man, Shakespeare said." He sat down, and smiled at me. "I'm glad we're able to talk."

"One thing's bothering me. Why the long silence? Why have Mum and you had no contact all these years? Why don't you even send me birthday cards?" I'd almost worked myself up into a state in which I'd soon feel tears at the back of my eyes. "Not even birthday cards," I repeated.

"Well . . ." He paused for a long time. "You could think this is self-justification . . . but I have to blame your mother entirely. No, blame is the wrong word. But it was your mother's doing. She was so hurt . . . she just wished to forget I ever existed. She didn't want to see me, speak to me, anything—except for getting the monthly cheque. She said she didn't need me 'contaminating' you. She felt you should grow up entirely free from such an influence. As if it was infectious, like bubonic plague . . ."

"I don't think anybody could turn me into . . . I mean, I've never thought I'd like to do something with another boy. Hmmm. I suppose it's possible."

"But not probable. Your sexual orientation is fixed by the time you're three or four, or earlier perhaps, even if, like me, it takes years to discover it."

"You could still have sent me a birthday card," I said.

"Yes. I could have done—*should* have done. I was trying to respect Nora's wishes. Guilt . . . feeling I ought to do whatever she wanted me to do. But she hasn't a monopoly, I guess, on what is right."

"She often thinks she has."

He looked at me, surprised. "Don't you two get along?"

"Yes, fine, I suppose. She's . . . she's Mum. I certainly couldn't talk to her like this."

He laughed, and said "I don't doubt it."

"Well . . . I'll . . . find something to eat. Are you sure you don't want any food?"

"Yes, I'm sure."

"I might go out later."

He waved an arm. "Do anything you like, short of getting into trouble."

"Mum would ask where I was going, and who with, and what time will I be back."

"I think I can trust you to be sensible, so there isn't a need to ask. Bournemouth's not exactly Sin City. You're . . . a good boy, Mike. Rather more mature than I'd have guessed."

"I don't feel very mature. I feel . . . muddled."

"One always does," he said.

"Isn't there a time when everything slots into place?"

"One thinks there is. But it's an illusion."

After I'd eaten—I found some cold chicken and salad in the fridge—I changed my clothes. I had a new tee-shirt, and a new pair of white trousers, and I spent a long time looking at myself in the mirror. Soon I'd have to shave every day. Something exciting would happen this evening, I told myself; I didn't know what exactly, but it would be . . . exciting.

I went round to Miranda's house. There was nobody in. Disappointed, I walked up the street to the main road, wondering what to do with myself. A bus came along, CITY CENTRE on its direction sign. Why not? I hadn't explored the centre of Bournemouth. I jumped on. But I didn't know where to go or what to do. I wished I wasn't sixteen. You aren't allowed into discos—unless they're organizing some special event for teenagers—or bars, and that leaves coffee shops, arcades with pinball machines, and hanging around on street corners. I had a coffee, then wasted thirty pence in an arcade. The excitement was still tingling inside me, but it was turning into frustration. What did I want? A girl. To be quite honest, sex: all the way.

The town had a keyed-up, holiday air. I watched people getting in and out of cars, going into pubs and clubs. But I was excluded, just as I was from the happy, happy families. There *is* no such thing as fairness. Why did Miranda have to be out? We could have gone for a walk on the cliffs, held hands, enjoyed the warm night wind and the flower scents, or paddled through the sea's edge in the dark. The tide was in, the waves churning restlessly round the legs of the pier, and crashing on the sand. They drifted gently back, re-formed, and curled over again. Courting couples in the shelters. A dog, sniffing at lamp-posts.

Waste of an evening. I decided to get rid of my surplus energy by walking all the way home; it took a good hour or more. The wind never stopped fretting the pine trees, slamming gates shut, blowing paper across the grass on the cliff tops, wailing in telephone wires.

Dad was there, sitting in the same armchair. The ash tray was full and the gin bottle empty. He was snoring. The stereo was on, the needle going back and forth in the centre of the Mahler record. I switched it off, drank the gin still left in his glass, turned out the lights and went to bed, leaving him where he was.

4. *Fear of flying*

He was still in the same chair next morning. "Oh, my head!" he moaned.

"Serve you right," I said, primly.

"I know, I know. I don't need my son to tell me that!"

During the next few days he kept off the bottle, but he was very depressed. He seemed shrunk, almost a husk of a man, the inside dried up. He talked little, and his movements were like a grandfather's—shuffling and slow. But his appetite was not affected by what had happened; he ate normally, enjoying to some extent, I think, cooking meals: if I hadn't been there, he said, he would probably have lived on snacks—sandwiches and soup. I began to realize that my being around was useful; if it didn't stop him brooding, it meant he was brooding less than if he had been alone. His chief complaint was that he couldn't sleep properly—he'd doze off all right at eleven or midnight, but wake at two or three in the morning, unable to sleep again. I never heard him during the small hours, but he would go to his study or lie in bed and read till I woke.

I tried to be there when he wanted my company, and he roused himself sufficiently one afternoon to propose a game of tennis on the local courts. He administered a good sound thrashing—6-1, 6-1. I was surprised at his agility and anticipation; although he was middle-aged he could run faster than me, and he always seemed to know exactly where I was trying to place the ball and put himself in the right spot to whack it miles out of my reach. He was muscular and wiry—he had the physique of a much younger man. Or so I thought. How do I know, I then said to myself, what the body of a forty-five-year-old looks like? Or a twenty-five-year-old? Apart from the obvious signs like a fat stomach, you guess people's age by their faces, not their bodies, which are almost invariably hidden by clothes.

He enjoyed winning the game, the first thing, apart from the cooking, that he did enjoy that week. "The older generation isn't on the way out yet!" he said, smiling.

"You should take that as a general sort of motto," I answered.

"Meaning what?"

"Adrian isn't the end of the world."

"Oh." His face clouded. "I should find somebody else, you're saying. Well . . . maybe. Maybe not. It might do me some good to live on my own for a while."

"I don't think so."

He laughed. "What do you know about it?"

"Nothing. But I was thinking of Mum. I reckon it hasn't done her a lot of good just living all these years with Aunt Bridie. She's still bitter . . . or so I guess; I don't know for sure."

"You're right. She should have found herself another man."

"In that case, so should you."

"Good God!" He grinned. "Sixteen-year-old advises father to find lover of same sex. What is the world coming to? Let's talk about tennis; it's not so embarrassing. You need practice, practice, practice. And your stance is quite wrong when you're hitting a forehand drive; no wonder it goes into the net so often. Don't face the ball; you need to put yourself almost ninety degrees to the right of where you usually stand." He manoeuvred me into the correct position. "And wait, before you hit it, till it's low; till it's dipping. Take it on the middle of the racquet, then wham! It'll sizzle over the net and kick up the chalk on the base-line."

"How can I possibly remember to do all that at once?"

"If you practise enough it becomes instinct. Watch how Connors and Borg do it."

And so on, most of the way home.

He didn't mention Adrian much, though I guess he wanted to. He probably thought it unfair to burden me with that subject, but one evening he said I mustn't think their life together had merely consisted of rows and ill-temper and Adrian contributing nothing. There had been some marvellous times. Moments of sheer magic. And he reminisced for a while about parties and mutual friends, holidays in California and the Greek islands, dancing at discos.

"Discos?" I was surprised at my father indulging in something I thought only kids would be interested in.

"Why not? You're not past it when you get to the age of twenty! Disco's the best kind of dance that's ever been invented. Oh, how I used to hate it when I was a teenager doing foxtrots and sambas and quicksteps! Always afraid I was going to tread on the girl's feet, or her dress, and feeling like an idiotic fool. Now . . . I can spend hours on the floor and relish every minute of it! Adrian's a very good dancer; it was always fun with him."

"You danced . . . together?" The idea of men dancing with men and enjoying it was really weird. I know boys dance with each other these days and don't get laughed at, but I'd always thought they did so because they were too shy to ask the girls.

"Of course we danced together," Dad said. He switched on the stereo and selected a record—Laura Branigan's *Gloria. Was it something that they said . . . or the voices in your head . . . Glory, Glor-i-a!* He did a few steps, then shouted over the music, "Come on! Dance with me!" I started to giggle. "What's

54

the matter?"

"With my father . . . it seems so peculiar!"

"Why? Haven't you ever danced with your mother?"

"No."

"Well . . . come on! The music will stop in a minute." I joined in. "Good, good!" He was most approving. "A natural sense of rhythm. Better than mine."

Our performance continued for over half an hour, to the accompaniment of Abba, the Beatles, Donna Summer and Diana Ross. "Golden oldies," Dad said. "They don't make them like this any more. All that awful Punk and New Wave; can't see anything in it."

"I need a drink," I said, eventually.

"The young have no stamina," he shouted, as I went into the kitchen and poured myself an orange juice; but, despite what he said, he was sitting in an armchair when I returned, puffing and panting.

These moments of relief from his general mood of sadness and depression were rare, however. There were times when he didn't want me around at all, so I took myself off to swim, or went to Miranda's house, or just walked about the streets. In the mornings he worked, or tried to, but the noise of the typewriter clacking away was infrequent. "I can't really do anything positive," he said. "My mind isn't on the job. If he's killed that, I'll go out and kill *him*!" He looked as if he meant it.

"Killed what?" I asked.

"Being able to write, of course! How else can I earn my living if that's gone? I'm supposed to finish this book by September, but . . . I don't know . . ."

One day when he was out grocery shopping, I went into Adrian's room and tried to play the harp—plucking one string at a time and listening to the note fade, then brushing my fingers rapidly to and fro in waterfalls of jangling discords. I hadn't any idea of how to produce a real tune, but I loved the quality of the sound—rich, fruity, mellow: it conjured up visions of gold-coloured wine, ancient castles, Irish chieftains, or dancers on a stage against a romantic misty backcloth of swans and lakes and mountains. Or something more indefinable, like sunlight, or the restless yearnings I felt in myself the evening I had wandered about the streets and walked all the way home along the edge of the sea. I wished the harp would just simply play itself, as it does in Jack and the Beanstalk, and give a perfect performance.

I looked up and saw Dad standing in the doorway, watching. In my concentration I had failed to listen for his return from the supermarket. "I thought . . . I thought for one moment Adrian was here," he said, stammering slightly. "But I realized, half way up the stairs, that he wouldn't be making those peculiar noises."

"I'm sorry. You told me not to touch it."

"It doesn't really matter. Now. But I'd rather you didn't when I'm in the house, if you don't mind. It . . . hurts."

I saw Miranda most days, and occasionally in the evenings. One night we went to the cinema, some stupid horror film: it was my suggestion; I thought if she really freaked out she'd want my arm round her, or my hand to hold. A friend at school had told me of this old trick. It paid off, very satisfactorily; and on the way home we found ourselves crossing the grass of the cliff top—I didn't organize it and neither did she, but that was where our footsteps took us. After about ten minutes she said "I think I'd better go home."

"Why?"

"I don't want you getting carried away."

"Where to?" There seemed to be an almost infinite number of possibilities.

"Don't be daft!" She walked to the road. I followed. "You aren't exactly the shy, backward type," she said, when I caught up with her.

"I've never done anything . . . sensational . . . with a girlfriend," I said. "If . . . girlfriend's the right word to use."

"I guess it is."

"I'm glad . . . you think I'm not the shy, backward type."

"I think . . ." She took a deep breath. "I think you're incredibly handsome, if you actually want to know."

"Thank you." My voice sounded faint, and my heart began to beat very quickly.

"The sort to take advantage of all the girls."

"I admit . . . I'd like to. With you."

She laughed. When we were outside her house, she gave me a peck on the cheek, and said "I'll see you tomorrow."

I went home, feeling quite pleased with the world. We had, in fact, become close friends over the past few days. I'd told her about the situation with Dad—everything. She wasn't shocked, as I'd more or less expected, but kind and sympathetic. A girl she knew at school was in a similar predicament, or at least had lived since the age of three with her mother and her mother's female lover. Maybe it wasn't as uncommon as I'd thought; I'd imagined my position was unique. My father, Miranda said, sounded interesting, quite unlike her own dad who, though he was the same age as mine, was *really* old—he spent all his spare time smoking his pipe and watching the telly. Boring! She'd read several of my father's books and enjoyed them, but she hadn't known he lived just round the corner. Perhaps she could bring them to the house and ask him to autograph them for her. I didn't encourage this idea; I'm not sure why—perhaps because in her company I

57

felt I was a normal teenage kid, whereas with Dad I felt very different: acting, or trying to act, an adult part in an off-beat script, the lines of which were still foreign to me. I just wasn't the same person, I thought. Though which was the more real me was a question I didn't bother to pursue; maybe because I was happy in both roles. Both, at least, were more worthwhile than the boy who played about at Alresford station and stopped trains from being derailed.

As events turned out, that was the last time I saw Miranda for almost a year.

Next morning, Dad seemed to have regained some of the energy he had when I first met him. He bustled around, hurrying through breakfast, and said he had to go out on an important errand. When I asked what it was, he told me, with a rather mysterious smile, that I'd have to wait and see. I went to Miranda's, but her mother said she was at the hairdresser's and wouldn't be back for a couple of hours. I decided to continue my wanderings round the streets.

It's difficult to say why I liked those streets so much. There was nothing particularly individual in their atmosphere; they looked the same, I imagine, as any other collection of roads in thousands of other places where fairly well-to-do people live in detached and semi-detached houses built in the nineteen thirties. The appeal was something to do with the gardens. I've never really done any gardening—Mum and Aunt Bridie were always content to leave ours as a desert, so they didn't instil into me or Nic much information about shrubs and plants—and perhaps because ours was such a perpetual wilderness (dandelions and ground elder were the chief examples of its produce), I got interested in other people's. I like a garden in which you can't see the edges, where trees hide fences, or walls are covered in clematis and jasmine, so you think it goes on for ever; and little paths meander away into the shadows and give the illusion of some secret, magical world hidden behind escallonia bushes or the forsythia hedge: Bournemouth was full of gardens like this. I imagined they belonged to people I'd like, content to let flowers and humans and things be themselves and do what they wanted to do. Someone who tolerated hollyhocks, shasta daisies, hydrangeas and red hot pokers sprawling out comfortably all over the place probably also tolerated kids sprawling out comfortably all over the place. The gardens I hate are those with plastic gnomes and no plant more than about one foot high—rigidly square creations in which you see fences more than the flowers, full of nothing but antirrhinums and salvias and pansies. The owners, I guess, are square rigid men and women who bully their kids into being exactly like themselves. Our neighbour at Alresford, Mrs Eggins, invariably refused to give us our ball back if Nic or I knocked it over the fence in a cricket game, and her garden was an eyesore. She had a flower bed with the words WELCOME TO ALRESFORD spelled out in purple petunias. Her children were just like her and the garden—nasty. As for Mrs Tope, whose garden led down to the railway embankment—she'd plant plastic daffodils in February, and tie red plastic balls on her apple trees in August, so the passengers on the train would think her flowers and her fruit were so well cared for that they appeared before any else's. She was crazy. As for the chaos of our own garden, I think it was a reflection of the fact that since Uncle John died and Dad left home, neither Mum nor Aunt Bridie have cared much about anything or anyone.

On my way home that morning I decided that the best garden in the whole district was at 8, Watcombe Road. As I was staring at its flowers and lily pond, a boy about the same age as myself came out of the front door of the house, carrying a surf board. He stared back—a long, lingering look not suspicious or hostile, but, like mine, just curious. Dad's garden was pretty good too, I thought, as I walked along the Overcliff Drive.

He was listening to a record—the Beethoven fourth piano concerto; much healthier than Mahler—but he turned it off when I appeared. "We're going away on a little trip," he said. He was grinning, and he had an air about him of suppressed excitement.

"Where to?" I asked, imagining he'd say Salisbury Cathedral or Stonehenge.

"Amsterdam."

"Amsterdam! But . . . that's in *Holland*!"

"Oh, eleven out of ten! My son isn't just a pretty face!"

"But . . . I haven't got a passport. Or any money. And . . . I've never been abroad."

"Well, it's high time you did go abroad," he said. "Your education has obviously been sadly lacking in a few basic essentials. Now, you don't have to worry about money, and as for a passport, we'll go to the post office after lunch and get you one of those temporary ones. You need a photograph, so we'll have to pop into that booth at the station and take some mug-shots."

Amsterdam! "Where will we stay?" I asked. It was bewildering . . . mad!

"In a hotel. It's all booked—I went to a travel agent in Southbourne this morning. Tomorrow afternoon at four p.m. we fly from Heathrow."

"Fly! In an aeroplane!"

"Well, it isn't on a bat's back."

"But I will be terrified!"

"Statistically, it's more probable that you'll be killed in a road accident." He brushed off my objections with a wave of the hand. I was beginning to learn a lot more about him, I decided with some alarm; he was a man who evidently liked doing wild things on the spur of the moment, and when he'd got an idea fixed in his head he bullied other people to go along with him. Was leaving Mum a sudden whim? Did Adrian get bullied? The depressed, hurt, unhappy dad of the past few days was easier to deal with than this. "The flight only takes an hour," he said. "You're no sooner up in the air than you're coming down again. You'll wish it wasn't so quick."

"I very much doubt it."

"Will you really be terrified?"

"Yes."

"Hmmm. Well, it can't be helped. It's all settled."

"How long are we going for?" I asked.

"A week."

"A week! That means . . . as soon as we get back, I'll have to go home."

"You can stay in this house for as long as you like. I'm . . ." He grinned, shyly. "I'm tremendously pleased you're here . . . It should have happened ages ago. And often."

"I think so too."

"I'm sorry about that. Adrian . . . Oh, never mind about Adrian."

"He didn't want me?"

"Er . . . no. Every time I suggested you should come and stay, he created a tantrum. Anyhow, your mother wouldn't have let you. It's only because you're growing up she agreed."

"He was jealous, I suppose."

"Was?" He sighed. "I guess was is right. He won't come back."

I walked about the room, agitated, trying to absorb all the information of the past few minutes. Until just now the only things occupying my mind were Bournemouth's gardens, and when Miranda would return from the hairdresser's. "Should I phone Mum," I asked, "and tell her what we're doing?"

"Why?"

"Won't she worry?"

"More likely to worry if she does know what we're doing. Besides . . . I seem to remember a clause in the divorce papers that says neither she nor I can whisk you out of the country without the other's consent. Probably written into it in case one of the parties tries to kidnap you. So . . . I'd better ask you . . . would you like to come to Amsterdam with me? We must make sure the whole thing is voluntary on your part." He laughed.

I laughed too. I was already captivated by his mood, and beginning to feel butterflies of excitement myself. Amsterdam! "Of course I'd love to come," I said. "God! Wait till I tell Nic about it! He'll be green with envy!"

"We'll have to get busy then; we're off at nine o'clock tomorrow morning on the London train from Pokesdown. You can put all your dirty clothes in the washing machine this afternoon; you don't want to get stuck for a week with only one pair of clean knickers. Lunch first." He removed the Beethoven, and replaced it with Irene Carra singing *Fame*, turned it up full blast and discoed out to the kitchen.

I followed him, and shouted over the din "Why Amsterdam?"

"Why not?"

"Why not Paris or Rome?"

"Often been to Amsterdam. It's beautiful! Canals and old houses and plenty of interesting things to do. You'll love it." He opened the fridge door, and took out some celery and a plate of tuna fish. "Help yourself; that's all there is today. Mike . . . I decided I needed a break. I need to get out of this house . . . get away from here." He shook his head. "Too many memories. I can't work; I just . . . Turn that damn thing down, will you? I can't hear myself speak. In fact, turn it off." I did so. "I just sit in my study," he said, "and look at the sea. I don't even *see* the sea when I look at it."

"Has he written, or phoned?"

"No." The excitement had vanished, like a burst bubble. "Still . . . to alter the old cliché, I may have lost a lover, but I've gained a son." He paused, thinking. "He'll write, I guess. When he needs his stuff. The harp. Etcetera."

"I don't know any Dutch," I said, trying to shift him back to a more cheerful subject.

"Neither do I," he answered, "but it doesn't matter. You hear English spoken more often than Dutch in the streets of Amsterdam. Now . . . if, when we're there, you want to go off and explore on your own, you must be careful about two things. Drug pushers, and—"

"I'm not into any drugs. I've never even smoked marijuana."

"I'm glad to hear it. Nasty, smelly substance."

"Have you smoked it?"

He looked taken aback at this question, and somewhat embarrassed. "Once or twice," he admitted. "But I don't want *you* doing it. Hmmm. That doesn't sound right, does it? Liberal, easy-going dad refused to let son do what he's done himself . . . These questions muddle me. I smoked it once or twice, as I said, just to see what it was like, but I was thirty-five at the time. It's the worry or the fear, I suppose, that kids of sixteen aren't old enough to know what they're getting into . . . Oh, hell, I find these conversations uncomfortable! It isn't like sex; a right age and a wrong age . . . but . . . anyway, Amsterdam is a very relaxed city. Lax, some people would call it. A lot of drugs change hands there, so I want you to be careful."

"I said I've never touched anything; I'm not interested." Then I added, mischievously, "What would you say is the right age for sex, then? Thirty-five?"

He stared at me almost angrily for a moment. "The other danger I have to warn you about is the red light district. It's rough and sleazy because in Holland prostitution is very open and above board. Too much so in my opinion—some of the streets in that area aren't safe to walk in. I think you're the kind of kid who can look after himself, but don't make any silly decisions, that's all. Anyway, as I told you, there are masses of interesting places to see and things to do."

We went to the post office and got my passport, then did some shopping. Dad bought jeans for both of us, then said he wanted a shirt and that a pair of sneakers was a dire necessity for me; my current pair was on the point of imminent collapse, which was true. Buying clothes restored his good mood; when we reached home he was as effervescent as a child let out of school. After tea, I rushed round to Miranda's house to tell her everything that had happened, but she wasn't in—gone to visit her aunt, Ben said, and he didn't know what time she would be back.

I was so tensed up that I slept badly, waking every so often from nightmares in which planes crashed to the ground, or caught on fire in mid-air and exploded. In the morning I had a headache which bothered me all the way up to London. Our route took us through Southampton and Winchester; when we stopped at Winchester I saw Mr Bowles's little engine sniffling and snorting at the next platform. I was afraid I might be seen by Mum, Aunt Bridie and Nic arriving on some spending spree, and I was relieved when our train started to glide out of the station. At Headbourne Worthy I had a brief glimpse of watercress beds, the wide, lazy River Itchen and its willows; and I wondered, with a pang of loss or longing, if I'd ever be delivered back to the safe, familiar world of Alresford and my childhood.

We travelled from Waterloo to Heathrow on the underground, so I didn't see much of London, a city I'd visited but didn't know a great deal about. One day, I said to myself, I will get to know it, better than anywhere else in the world . . . Now the airport, and I couldn't decide whether I was more frightened than bewildered, more excited than worried. It was huge! Everything was on a grand scale—the buildings, the runways, the aeroplanes themselves, the noise, and particularly the long, slow progress from the baggage check-in through passport control, the duty-free shops and the innumerable lounges and corridors to the departure gate.

The plane was a lot bigger than I had expected, though Dad said it was only a 727, quite small compared with the monster-size jumbos that flew across the Atlantic and half-way round the world to Australia and New Zealand. "This trip is like getting on a bus," he said. "Just an hour's ride." It didn't seem like a bus to me. "Are you going to be all right?"

"I shall have to be," I said. "There's not much I can do about it now."

"You can get off and take the train home."

There hadn't been much I could do about it from the start, I thought, and I wondered again if Dad always got his way so easily with other people. Our seats were at the back, which helped—I remembered reading of a plane crash in which the only survivors were the passengers in the tail: on impact with the ground, the tail had conveniently snapped off, and was the one bit of the wreck not to become an instant fiery furnace.

I refused Dad's suggestion of a place by the window. "You'll see more from there," he said. "And I've seen it all before."

"I think I'll feel happier if I don't look out of the window."

Take-off was terrifying. The speed with which we surged forward, much faster than any car or inter-city train, almost embedded me into the seat, and the roar and the jolting, though not as bad as I had feared, were sufficient to set the adrenalin racing—my palms sweated; my throat was dry and my stomach was a tight knot. Then we were in the air. Just like that: one moment careering over tarmac at heaven knows how many hundred miles an hour, about to smash to pieces, so I thought, in the houses at the edge of the airport; the next rising above them, the plane dipping its starboard wing to make a turn, so that the roads and railways and buildings of West London—I couldn't help but look, although I'd said I wouldn't—were like an ordnance survey map I was holding vertically at the side of my face, instead of putting it horizontally on a table. Then we were in the clouds—exactly as if we were immersed in dense fog—then above them, with the sun shining down on a vast mattress, it seemed, of fluffy cotton wool. It actually appeared to be quite safe; it gave me the illusion that, if the plane suddenly dropped, we would just bounce on some kind of celestial trampoline. The no-smoking lights were switched off, and there was no need any longer for seat belts. People unclunked and unclicked, lit cigarettes, got up and moved about as if they really were doing something utterly normal like travelling, as Dad had said, on a bus—well, maybe a train—instead of taking part in the most unnatural activity I could imagine human beings indulging in: whizzing through the air at immense speed thousands of feet above solid earth.

"O.K. now?" Dad asked.

"Yes," I said, smiling. I was.

"Want to sit by the window?"

"Might as well, I suppose. Thanks."

We changed places. "We're already over the North Sea," he said. "You can glimpse it through the holes in the cloud."

There it was: a wrinkled sheet, and an oil tanker sat on it; absolutely stationary it looked, with the V of its wake behind it like a crease. "Do they give us any food?" I asked. On air journeys, I knew, free drinks were provided, and dinners in plastic boxes.

"Not on a flight as short as this," he said. "There wouldn't be time to serve it. But do you want something? I can speak to one of the stewardesses."

"No. It's all right." I felt disappointed. "I wish they hadn't shown us that stuff about oxygen masks and emergency exits," I said.

"Just as well to know where the escape hatches are."

"Yes, I agree. But telling you all that somehow implies they're expecting the worst."

"Oh . . . nonsense!" He started to read a magazine he had brought with him; he was evidently losing any sympathy he might have felt—not much to begin with—for my stupid fear of flying. This fear was, in fact, fast evaporating, like the thinning cloud beneath us: the sea was quite clear now, and a long stretch of sand. A beach: behind it houses and fields. Holland! I thought of windmills and tulips, and Dutch girls in clogs, and landscape so flat that nothing appeared to happen in it except in the far distance. (Well, that was the impression I had got from prints of Dutch paintings.)

The pilot's voice came over the intercom. "We are now beginning our descent to Amsterdam Schiphol. Please fasten your safety belts and extinguish your cigarettes." Dad was right, as usual: it had been unbelievably quick.

The sensation of coming down was far from pleasant, and my terror returned, though not so acutely as when we had taken off. We re-entered the cloud, and the engine noises altered; there were all sorts of little bumps and trembles, and the wing—what I could see of it—seemed to be shaking. Suppose another plane was flying about in this murk and the pilot didn't know? Radar, I reassured myself, and the airport control people were talking us down—they knew what else was charging round up here. But I was glad when we broke through the cloud and I could see another squashed-eyeball view of ordnance map buildings and roads and fields, looking, alas, much like the version we'd left behind in England.

Ca-rump! Only the smallest of jolts as we touched the runway, then once more we were belting along tarmac at petrifying speed. Slowing, however, with every second that passed. When the plane stopped, people unclunked again, then stood up to take their luggage from the storage compartments overhead. I gazed out of the window. Certainly the landscape was flat, but where were the windmills and the Dutch girls in clogs? (It was the wrong time of year for tulips, of course.) This airport looked much the same as Heathrow— concrete and glass. Maybe all airports are similar. But the city of Amsterdam, I hoped, would not be like anything in Britain.

We'd arrived! Excitement replaced fear, as I told myself this would be the first time I'd ever set foot on foreign soil. (Scotland, I decided, didn't count.)

5. Amsterdam

On the rundfahrt—what a rude language Dutch is! In fact it means *round trip* and I discovered later that the word is borrowed from German—I realized that Amsterdam was not only a very beautiful city, but one that demanded exploration on my own. Not exactly as Bournemouth had done (it couldn't possibly have been more different) but because it was a city of young people: every bridge, every square, every street market had crowds of kids. Bournemouth was mostly what my father had called it—costa geriatrica. The rundfahrt was a trip by water; Amsterdam was a little like my mental pictures of Venice, the city of canals. The boat took a tortuous route—left, right, left, left again, and so on—so that I completely lost my sense of direction. On the edges of the canals were cobblestone lanes, many of them planted with big leafy trees, and on their far sides were terraces of tall seventeenth and eighteenth century houses, built of brick so mellowed with time that they seemed to have been there for ever, each one individual in its paintwork, its pattern of windows, the ornamentation on its gables, the design of its front door, and all leaning together as if, with age, they needed their neighbours' support to prevent them from toppling into the canals. Every so often an alley or a narrow passage opened up, revealing at its end something of interest that beckoned me, a tree in sunlight, a square with people milling about, a man playing a barrel organ, the walls of an ancient church. I just wanted to be by myself and soak up the atmosphere. But as soon as another new scene was revealed, the boat chugged on, removing whatever it was and replacing it with the next vista, only to snatch that away also. It was like being shown all the goodies in a sweetshop, but being told not to touch any of them.

Out hotel, on the Kerkstraat, was pleasant and old-fashioned; the staff were friendly and most of them spoke English. A Dutch breakfast was a bit odd—a lot of it seemed to consist of cheese—but the coffee was excellent, and so were the various kinds of bread. My father took me to the art galleries—the Rijksmuseum and the Van Gogh Museum— and on our second evening we went to the Concertgebouw to hear Amsterdam's world-famous orchestra. "Much more famous than the Wessex," Dad said, "and I promise you there will be no Mahler." The music I enjoyed this time, though my thoughts wandered in the slow passages—Mendelssohn's *Overture to A Midsummer Night's Dream*, Debussy's *Nocturnes*, and the *London Symphony* of Vaughan Williams. This culture was fine with me, and so was dinner at the bistro just across the way from our hotel, which served English food: pork chops and salad, roast beef and runner beans.

But I was restless; I wanted something more than a tour, conducted by Dad, of music, works of art, and trips by boat to look at buildings. At breakfast on our third morning, when he asked me what I'd like to do, I said "Can I just go off on my own for a few hours?" I wondered if I should have kept silent, for he didn't appear to be in too happy a mood, and I did not want to upset him, particularly when he was so concerned to give me a good time.

He thought for a moment, then said "Make a day of it, if you wish."

"Are you sure?"

"I'll give you a street map—I've got one in our room and I've marked the hotel with an X. I'd better write down the phone number, so you can ring here if you're lost. Come back at . . . tea-time. Five o'clock. No later than six. I'd like to eat tonight at an Indonesian restaurant I know, the other side of town. Do you need some money?"

"I've thirty guilders."

"Well, that should buy you something for lunch, and leave plenty to spare. Watch out for bicycles."

"Bicycles?"

"You must have noticed, what with the canals and the rabbit warren of little streets, that this is not a city for cars. It's impossible to drive here! Good thing too. Everyone walks or takes a tram or rides a bike. You can be run over by madcap cyclists more easily than being knocked down by a car. And . . . if you get on a tram, you pay at once. It isn't like an English bus, with the conductor coming round for the fares. The driver could be rather shirty if you walked past him without paying; he'd think you were trying to defraud the tram company. Well . . . enjoy yourself."

"Thanks Dad; I will. This Indonesian restaurant . . . do you think I'll like that kind of food?"

"Mike, how on earth should I know?" He really did sound irritable this morning; Adrian was obviously on his mind again. "All I can do as your father," he said, "is to present you with things and people and places; put you in front of them and say 'I like this, or I enjoy that, or I approve of the other' and hope you'll agree. But *you* have to decide whether you agree. Or not."

"What will you do with yourself while I'm gone?"

"No need to worry about that. I'll stroll about . . . have a drink at a café, read the newspaper. Go to the sauna, probably."

"The sauna? You come all the way to Amsterdam to go to a sauna?"

"Like coming all the way here to sit in a café and read the newspaper?" A smile hovered at the corners of his mouth. "I enjoy saunas. They're very relaxing."

"What do you do in there?"

"Sit stark naked on a bench in stifling heat."

"Men *and* women?"

He laughed. "Sorry to ruin your fantasies. No."

"Ah. I get it. It doesn't sound like fun to me."

He raised an eyebrow, and said "Off you go now, and have a good time. If we bump into one another, I'll buy you a drink."

Sagittarius is my birth-sign, and though I don't believe in all that astrology nonsense, my mother says Sagittarians are born wanderers, the world's travellers; and as far as women are concerned, the males of this sign love them and leave them. Mum and Aunt Bridie are deeply into this sort of thing—casting horoscopes and reading the tarot pack and interpreting lines on the palms of people's hands. I haven't much experience of loving and leaving girls, but I'm certainly a born wanderer. Mum's a Virgo—icky picky typey, Aunt Bridie says; their role at parties, she says, is to empty the ash-trays. Dad's a Taurus, but I don't know him well enough yet to find out if he has the Bull's characteristics. Maybe I'll ask him. Anyway, to get back to me and wandering, I took to Amsterdam as happily as I did to Bournemouth, which I knew on the rundfahrt I would.

The weather was perfect. Sunlight glittered on the canal waters; it was hot, and a gentle breeze prevented the air from becoming too muggy. I turned off the Kerkstraat into a busier road—trams and dozens of cyclists; Dad was definitely right about the possibility of being knocked down by a bicycle. I strolled through the flower market—all the same flowers that one might buy, or see in gardens, in England in August; there were even a few early chrysanthemums and kaffir lilies. Then over a canal into a part of the city where the streets were narrower and more winding; it was an area

72

of print shops, second-hand jewellers, and book stores. I studied my map: Amsterdam was shaped a bit like an onion sliced in half—the main canals were built, more or less, in a series of semi-circles, and I was walking from the outer rings to the centre, the oldest quarter of the city. The Dutch must be a nation of avid readers, I thought, particularly in foreign languages, for the number of book-shops was prodigious, and most of them had a section of books in German or French or English. Some of these places were of the pornographic variety; quite unlike anything I'd seen in the streets of Winchester. I went inside one, expecting to be told I was too young to be allowed in. I don't look any older than I actualy am, or younger for that matter—just plain sixteen. As I said before, it's not a good age to be, even if a girl like Miranda thinks I'm incredibly handsome. I'm not incredibly handsome—tall, very bony, with ordinary curly black hair and ordinary green eyes. At sixteen most people look down at you if you go on playing children's games, but at the same time they think you aren't old enough to indulge in the adult activities you want to indulge in. Dad seemed to be encouraging me to grow up, was in a way granting me a licence to stretch my wings; whereas Mum, I felt, still encapsulated me in a world of childhood. Which meant that last week—and maybe next, I thought gloomily—I was fiddling around on the railway lines at Alresford, and this week I was in a pornographic bookshop in Amsterdam staring at lewd pictures.

Nobody ordered me out, which shows perhaps that in Holland people have the good sense not to try and protect you from growing up. Some of the magazines were undoubtedly revealing, though I learned nothing I didn't know already. I thought of Dad's remark about silly decisions, and on the strength of that I did not waste my money on buying one; and I went out into the sunshine feeling not corrupt or depraved, but rather virtuous.

By lunch-time I'd seen a man swallowing fire and a juggler throwing knives (there was street entertainment everywhere, watched by large, appreciative crowds of tourists); refused the offer to share a joint with a gang of German kids I got talking to on one of the bridges; gazed at the outside of the royal palace in the Dam, a pretty modest effort, I thought, compared with the size of Buck House; and enjoyed lots of window shopping. There were shops that sold nothing but clogs, and I tried on a pair; klompen, I learned, was clogs in Dutch, a lovely-sounding word, very appropriate for the objects it described. But I didn't buy any; I'd never wear them—they were too uncomfortable. My only purchase was a little windmill, made of blue and white Delft china, in a shop that sold all sorts of Delft souvenirs—human figures in traditional Dutch costume, and tiles, as well as the normal things you'd expect in such a place, like mugs and vases and dishes. I hadn't yet seen a real windmill, so I reckoned a china one wasn't a bad substitute. Then I went into the Oudekerk (the old church); I'd been attracted to it because of the strange and beautiful music its bells played four times an hour, on the quarters, the half, and the hour itself. It reminded me of Adrian's harp. Amsterdam, in fact, was a city full of sweet, musical noises. On the pavements men played barrel organs, fantastic, ornate machines that churned out the old creaking sounds of old creaking tunes, like ghosts of carousels from ancient fairs. The church was incredibly quiet after the hubbub of the streets. Tall, whitewashed walls and silence.

A ham sandwich and a seven-up was my mid-day meal, then a slice of delicious sticky lemon cake I bought in a patisserie which at home would have been the best cake shop in town, but here was just one out of dozens I'd seen. I'd get fat if I lived in Amsterdam. I wandered on, over a canal that had been filled in and concreted, past another church that was standing, curiously, right in the middle of a road, and into a very different sort of area. I glanced up at the street name—Zeedijk—then at my map, which showed I was in the middle of the onion, the oldest bit of the city, the ground on which it had started centuries ago. There were a lot of rough men prowling about, but nothing too dreadful, I felt, could happen to me during the day. I turned into an alley; I'd seen a wide canal and a bridge at the end—it would lead me, presumably, out of the onion's centre. And I knew immediately that this was the red light district: it was so blatant. The women, wearing as few clothes as they possibly could, stood in the windows—big, plate glass windows—of little ground-floor apartments, and smiled and beckoned. It was embarrassing, but at the same time—exciting. I wanted to look: were they attractive? But not be observed. One of them said, in English, "Why don't you come inside?" She wasn't a great deal older than me.

So *that* is what it is all about, I said to myself.

I found a rare patch of grass by the side of the road—rare, because public gardens and parks did not exist in Amsterdam's inner city, and what blossom there was could only be seen in window boxes or cut, ready for sale, in the flower market—and I sprawled out on my back, staring up at the sky. I tried to make my mind go blank but it wouldn't—it was full of conflicting jumbled thoughts, like the clothes spinning round in a washing machine; Dad and Adrian and Mum and Nic and Miranda, Alresford and Bournemouth and Amsterdam. And sex, and silly decisions. Why did life become so complicated and contradictory as I got older? I spent most of my childhood wanting to grow up, and now I'd arrived, or nearly arrived, nothing was straightforward any more. Wasn't there one single pleasure I could have that would make me entirely happy, even if it was for just a brief while? Apparently not.

The absence of flowers here made me think about gardens. Like the pensioners of Bournemouth, I felt I wanted to make a garden. Maybe that's what I would do when I went home to Alresford; Mum and Aunt Bridie couldn't possibly object as they left Tralee so derelict. I tried to picture the grounds of our house when I'd finished with them, but the only image that would come into my head was the concert hall, the Winter Gardens. Growing up should be like passing from winter gardens into summer gardens, I thought, but maybe one of those places was just a more complicated version of the other, with mazes and paths that led nowhere. Or did they lead eventually round some unforeseen corner to exactly everything I'd always wanted? Whatever everything I'd always wanted might be; my ideas about that were totally vague.

The Indonesian meal was excellent. A rijsttafel, lots of small dishes like a Chinese dinner—chicken with almonds and peppers, shrimp, beef, sweet and sour pork, bean shoots—but the flavours were much more subtle than anything I'd get in a take-away in Winchester. Dad was in a good mood; the sauna had obviously cheered him up. "It unwinds you," he said, when I asked him if he'd enjoyed it. "Cleanses you. All your muddled thinking evaporates. Then I sat in the most enormous jacuzzi I've ever seen."

"What's a jacuzzi?"

"A hot tub, a bubble bath. It was big enough to accommodate a hundred people in comfort. Positively Roman."

"So you're feeling better?"

He laughed. "I certainly am!"

"Are you a typical Taurus, Dad?"

"That rubbish! But, well, if you like . . . yes, I could be. Obstinate, not too sensitive, fond of routine. And a glutton for the good things of life. On the plus side, artistic, creative, hard-working . . . and faithful, believe it or not. Why?"

"Oh, I just wondered."

"The wanderer wondered. How was Sagittarius's day? Typical?"

I leaned back in my chair, my hands behind my head. "I had a good time," I said, and I mentioned the Oudekerk, the fire-eater and the juggler, the cake shop, and the royal palace. Then, emboldened by a second glass of wine, I told him about the alley off the Zeedijk.

Expressions of astonishment and concern flitted across his face. "What do you expect me to say? I imagine you're aware of the risks in places like that. Disease. Robbery. But . . . have you ever considered it's degrading to women?"

I thought about that for a moment, then said "No."

"Perhaps you should consider it, then."

"I read somewhere that desire is an appetite. Like hunger. It needs satisfying."

"Rather more satisfying if *both* parties want it and they're in love." He pushed his empty plate away. "I've never done anything like that in my life," he said, and he looked a bit disgusted.

"Are you . . . angry?"

"Listen . . . you were curious, which is normal. But if a man spent all his time paying money for that, I'd say there was something radically wrong with him. There are better ways of fulfilling oneself as a sexual being, *and* of spending one's guilders."

"Yes. I'd already worked that out."

"Good."

"Like this food, the girl was Indonesian."

He sighed. "A poverty-stricken immigrant, and

because of economic distress . . . You know, the whole history of the world is about men demeaning women. Sir Matthew Hale, who was the Lord Chief Justice in the seventeenth century, said it was impossible for a man who raped his wife to be guilty of that crime, because—quote—'by their mutual matrimonial consent and contract, the wife hath given up herself in this kind unto her husband, which she cannot retract'. In other words, he believed a man can do what he wants with his wife and she has no say in the matter. Deplorable. Women, Michael, are *not* objects to be used."

I felt uncomfortable, and I had no answer, as so often with what he said. I almost resented the fact that he ran verbal rings round me with such ease. I decided to change the subject, and asked "What did Mum feel . . . when you left her?"

"Not a used object, if that's what you're implying."

"No. No, I wasn't . . . I was just interested."

He lit a cigarette, helped himself (but not me) to more wine, and said "You're entitled to know, and I'm surprised Nora hasn't told you. I didn't leave her, in the way those brutal little words always suggest when they're uttered by ignorant people. 'She ran off with another man.' 'He walked out on her.' As if the break-up of *any* relationship is as simple as walking out of a door! Our problem . . . *my* problem, that of being married and gay . . . it wasn't something we could reach a compromise about. Though we did a lot of talking at the time . . . for weeks on end; I was searching for a whole variety of possible solutions that would *not* destroy the marriage. She was adamant that I should go. I didn't want to; it was the last thing I wanted! But she was right. I saw that eventually."

"Was there anybody else involved?"

"You mean did I have a lover? No."

"Why was Mum so adamant?"

"She did what she did believing it was the best thing

for her and you. She was very much motivated by observing other marriages in which the husband and wife stayed together for the sake of the children, even though there was nothing left of love or affection between the two adults. She thought it was dreadful for kids to be brought up in such an atmosphere, and I agree with her. She was wrong, however, to see me as a contaminating influence . . . absurd!"

"None of this makes any difference," I said, "to the fact that I've missed out."

"Do you think," he asked, "you'd have been a better person—a happier, more fulfilled person—if I'd been there all the time?"

"I can't possibly know the answer to that! Can I?"

He refused to be deflected from this line of questioning, however, and said "What do you feel it *has* done to you?"

I thought about that for a while, then said "A friend of mine at school summed me up, not long ago, as intelligent, inquisitive, full of life—but cold. I didn't have much feeling. We were talking about the fact that I've never fallen in love, and that he had."

His eyes widened. "In love?"

"I'm sixteen! Why not?"

"Good Lord, it isn't something that happens to everybody at the same age! It isn't like doing 'O' levels! There really isn't a law that says because you're thirteen, or twenty, or fifty-seven, you've got to have done X or Y. It makes me angry—all those competitive parents turning their kids into more little competitors! 'My Willie could walk at ten months.' 'Samantha was potty-trained at nine months.'" I laughed; he was good at putting on ludicrous voices. "'Stephen began piano lessons at three!' And so on. Does the kids untold harm."

"In what way?"

"They learn to think life is one great big race to the

top. So they spend all their years kicking other people aside instead of forming real friendships and good relationships and healthy marriages. Don't be someone like that, Mike."

I was afraid I already was. I tried to turn the conversation back to a question I'd asked but which he hadn't answered. "What did Mum *feel* when you left?"

The waiter brought the bill, and Dad studied it, frowning. "The end of the world," he said. "I don't know if she's ever got over it. *I* have. Yes . . . it's much easier to be the one who departs than the one who stays, though at the time I thought the opposite. Events proved otherwise."

"Now *you're* the one who stays."

He finished his coffee, and counted his guilders. "You're referring to Adrian?"

"Yes. And I think . . . you'll get over it more easily than Mum did."

"You know what your trouble is?" he said. "You're too damned smart."

"You're still sleeping badly."

"How do you know?"

"I hear you." We shared a bedroom at the hotel, and every night this week he had woken in the small hours, hunted in the dark for a book to read, then crept downstairs. At dawn I would hear him return. He never disturbed me so much that I couldn't get back to sleep, and on the whole I enjoyed being in the same room with him. It was intimate, in a pleasant kind of way, as if he didn't object to what we saw of each other—both of us wandering around in the nude, for instance. Parents—Mum and my aunt were typical examples—always seem to hide themselves from their children, hide what they really think or feel, or their bodies; how much they earn, or the fact that Grandpa was a penniless photographer, which means you end up not wanting to be close to them, to confide in them. Dad was an extraordinary exception.

"The whole thing hasn't properly hit me yet," he said, as we left the restaurant. "Your visit, these few days here . . . they're helping to postpone looking at it all squarely in the eye. I won't know what Adrian's absence does to me until you've gone home to Alresford. As for now . . . well, I've sometimes sat in that hotel lounge not seeing the words on the page I'm reading. When I come back to bed, it's very reassuring to observe your sweet innocent face on the pillow."

"Sweet innocent face! Huh!"

"I say to myself 'that's my son!' With a . . . a . . . a sense of joy, almost. And I think . . . now you'll decide, probably with a lot of truth, that I'm indulging in self-justification . . . I think being a father isn't necessarily having to be physically present the whole time, making model aeroplanes or doing your maths homework, not at your age. It's a *feeling*. A kind of love."

Being a son, too, was a kind of love. That friend who'd told me I was cold was wrong. I could feel love, too. "Thank you," I said, "for talking like this . . . and for letting me talk."

He grinned, then looked away from me, suddenly shy and embarrassed. "Shall we go back to the hotel? There's a chess set in the lounge. Do you play?"

"For my school, as it so happens."

"We'll see if your ability at chess is better than your skill on the tennis court."

It was. I beat him twice, and the third game ended in stalemate.

The remainder of the week passed all too quickly. I spent much of it wandering, and thought I should never tire of Amsterdam's street life. I went on a conducted tour of the royal palace, but that was my only organized piece of culture. Dad visited the sauna several times, bought lots of books, and found new restaurants to eat in. Some days we spent together; we went on a train ride to Delft one afternon and saw the tombs of the Dutch royal family—very unfussy and simple I thought, and though the only British royal tomb I'd seen was equally unfussy (William the Second's black sarcophagus in Winchester Cathedral) I imagined some of our monarchs were fitted out in rather more lavish splendour than Queen Wilhelmina in Delft. I liked the train journey: it was a pleasant surprise to find the Dutch used their railways more than we did in England; the platforms were crowded, and the trains frequent. I bought a postcard of Delft Station and sent it to Nic.

On Friday it was good bye; the bus journey to Schiphol Airport, a long walk round the duty-free shop—"the biggest and best in the world," Dad said, as he stocked up on incredibly cheap gin and cigarettes, and a camera for me—then the renewed terrors of the plane taking off, the brief flight, and a dull, drizzly London.

"I have to go home tomorrow," I said. "I don't want to."

"Why do you *have* to?" Dad asked. "Some important date?"

"No."

"Stop another week. Stop as long as you like."

"But what would Mum say about that?"

"You'll have to ring and get permission."

"Hmmm."

"I'm not going to do it for you."

"I'll think about it," I said.

"We could improve your tennis. And my chess. You can swim, or see your girlfriend while I try to bang out a few paragraphs on the typewriter. We could go to another concert . . . though on second thoughts I'd rather steer clear of the Winter Gardens. Drive to

Poole or Salisbury or the New Forest, as I suggested once before and we never did. Whatever you want."

"I'll ring her."

When we opened the front door, Dad said immediately "Someone's been in here." Burglars? It all looked quite normal to me, but I didn't know the house as well as he did; if an object had been moved or was missing, he'd realize at once. On the kitchen table was a letter. "Adrian," he said, picking it up. "You make your phone call."

Mum was not pleased when she heard my request. "I thought this would happen," she said. "I shouldn't have let you go down there in the first place."

"Why?" I said, hotly. "He's my father and I have a right to see him!"

"He has too much charm. Too much influence."

"You've nothing whatever to worry about if you're imagining he could influence me into being homosexual!"

There was a very silent silence, as if the fearful word itself had killed her stone dead. "How much longer do you intend to stay?" she asked, faintly.

"Another week."

"Well . . . that's it then, a week and no more. I want you back here next Friday afternoon. I . . . hope, Michael, I'll find the same person who left here a fortnight ago."

"I haven't been corrupted or depraved. Not even mildly shocked . . . I've been having a nice time, and I'd like it to go on for a bit. We've . . . just returned from a few days in Holland."

"Holland! you mean . . . *Holland!* Whatever were you doing there?"

"Going abroad for the first time."

"Yes . . . well . . ."

"How's Aunt Bridie?"

"Got stung by a bee. Otherwise O.K."

"And Nic?"

"Camping out in that disgusting old fulling mill! Can't imagine why she allows it; that bee-sting must have turned her brains. Mike . . . look after yourself. I worry about you."

"There's nothing to worry about! I'll see you on Friday."

6. A family reunion

Adrian had returned to collect some of his property—
twenty-two things in all; everything else that was his, or
which he owned jointly with my father, he did not
want. The letter was a kind of formal acknowledgment
that the entire contents of the house—with the exception
of the harp, which was still in the room upstairs—now
belonged to Dad. Dad didn't let me read the letter, but
he told me the gist of it. "It makes life a bit simpler, I
suppose," he said. "One of the problems when a
relationship ends is who owns what. People can get
very unpleasant—arguing about who paid for the paint
on the toilet walls, or the fablon on the larder shelves.
This, for instance—" he tapped the kitchen table
"—belongs to both of us. Did. It would be rather a
nuisance having to go out and buy a new table and
chairs."

"What happened," I asked, "when you and Mum
broke up?"

"She had more or less everything. Even if I'd taken
half the stuff, I wouldn't have been able to put it
anywhere—I moved into a bedsit. Where I wrote my
first novel, as it so happens. Luckily the publisher took
it. I dread to think what would have occurred if I'd
never had a book accepted—still living in that room, I
imagine, or another one rather like it, teaching the less
able idiots in a comprehensive school how to punctu-
ate, and suffering from alcoholic depression." He filled
the kettle and put it on the stove. "Do you want a cup
of tea?"

"Please. Mum once said she wished she hadn't taken

all the furniture."

"Why?"

"It kept too many memories churning around, she said. She sold a lot of it four years ago . . . when Uncle John died and we moved in with Aunt Bridie and Nic."

"Did she?" Dad looked annoyed. "She could have asked me if *I* wanted some of it. There was a nice cane chair—peacock chairs they're called; you know the sort? With the huge back. I owned that . . . oh, years before I even met your mother."

I laughed. "It's in good hands. It lives in my bedroom at Tralee, and I'm very fond of it."

"Well, in that case . . . you know, Nora's probably right about the memories. I'm going to experience that here." He stared, unseeing, for a moment at the kettle, then said "Maybe I should sell up. Move to . . . no, this is stupid . . . Why should I let that man drive me out of my house?"

"What else did he say in his letter?"

"Nothing. It's just cold and business-like. How *can* he . . . ?"

We drank our tea in silence.

Later, I went round to Miranda's, but there was no answer when I knocked. The woman next door, who was trimming the hedge between the two gardens, peered over and said "They're away on holiday, in Cornwall. They won't be back for another two weeks." They never mentioned it to me, I said to myself, as I walked off. Very strange. Even if it was some sudden decision, like our trip to Amsterdam, she could have left me a note—slipped it through Dad's letter-box before she left. Maybe she gave it to Adrian, who forgot, or deliberately threw it in the dustbin. No . . . there was probably some reasonable explanation. But I couldn't help feeling more than a little sad, as I turned into the Overcliff Drive and stood on the grass to look at the sea. We had stood here, looking at it, the *two* of us.

The weather was changing. There was a strong wind, and the water was dark and hungry. Clouds were building up in the south-west, spires and towers and turrets, above Durlston Head. Waves were breaking much further out than usual, curling over and collapsing in white frothy anger. No one was swimming. People were collecting up their possessions, wrapping bathing costumes in towels, putting the remnants of picnics into bags and baskets; but a few tough beach-goers were refusing to let the weather disturb them, and they sat contentedly, watching the waves and the sky. I went down the cliff and squatted on the sand, resting my chin on my knees. It's the only place I can sit and do nothing, a beach—the sea, more than anything I can think of, satisfies the senses: the salt tangy smell, the constantly shifting pattern of noises, the slip and slither and flux that please the eye so much that there is no urge to stare elsewhere. And knowing that you're on the edge of civilization, the last point of land, is always exciting, though why that is I can't fathom. The sea was rushing in, pushing, receding, pushing: lacy surfaces of water obliterating sandcastles, almost convincing the watchers that soon it would engulf everything. The clouds, too, were hurtling towards us. I stayed where I was until the first light drops of rain were needles on my skin; then walked up the cliff path and reached home just before the deluge began.

"A summer storm," Dad said. "Was that lightning?" A distant rumble of thunder answered his question. He was preparing our evening meal—belly of pork with stewed apricots, a bit adventurous for him. As if he could read my thoughts, he said "Yes, I've decided to learn how to be a chef. I can't accept dinner invitations and not give proper meals in return; I'd lose all my friends. Adrian has left a whole shelf of cookery books—he must be crazy! So I'm experimenting on you. Pass me that jar of basil, please."

"Father accused of poisoning son," I said. "Something nasty in the apricots."

"A woman in Shakespeare died of poisoned apricots. Or was it in Webster? *The Duchess of Malfi*, perhaps . . . My memory is not what it was. Mmmm." He tasted the contents of the stew-pan. "Needs a little white wine."

A very mercurial person, my father. Introspective and listless one moment, then the next happily absorbed in some activity—tennis, Dutch royal tombs, apricots. Perhaps that was the secret I was looking for: always to have a glut of occupations to satisfy the mind. "It smells good," I said.

"How was your girlfriend?" he asked.

"Gone away on holiday."

"Oh. Well . . . you'll soon meet another girl. Though that can be more easily said than done, I suppose. You know, I wouldn't want to be sixteen again, but I envy you having the good things of life ahead to discover. Shame one can't do it all a second time, knowing what one knows now."

"Do you really mean that?"

"Of course not! There's a certain age—the forties—when you know and you still can. A very good age to be."

"Well, work on it." He looked puzzled, so I said "When you feel depressed."

He sighed. "I should. I can still do everything just as well as I did twenty years ago. Disco dance the whole night. Run about in shorts, as I am now, and not be ashamed of my legs." It sounded to me as if he wasn't absolutely convinced of all this; was he trying to reassure himself that he wasn't old, yet feeling that he was? Maybe there's an age when you know you can't start again: Dad's age. He could, as he grew older, get very lonely; if he didn't have someone to live with at forty-five, then perhaps he never would. He's lucky *I* exist. Was that the reason he was making such an effort to impress me, to be sure I liked him? A sort of insurance policy for his retirement? I dismissed the idea. He was just being himself: I could take it or leave it.

More lightning, and the thunder rolled fiercely overhead. The rain was torrential. "The flowers are going to be smashed to pieces," I said, looking out at the garden.

"Something pleasant and comfortable about a summer storm when you're *inside* the house. Listening to rain battering on the roof and knowing the roof doesn't leak. This pork is cooked . . . Let's see if it's edible."

More chess later. His game was slower and careful, but I still managed to win. By the end of the week it would be a different story; he was learning how to read my chess mind. As I ought to learn how to read his tennis mind, but couldn't, as the basic techniques I had were far inferior to his.

In Amsterdam he'd complained about people being competitive, that it ruined friendships. Yet he and I were competitive—very much so. I wanted to match him, be his equal, and he wanted to stay ahead. I wondered if at some future date it might spoil what was between us, or would he gradually relinquish things to me? Wasn't that the idea of having children—they should ultimately be your replacements? Perhaps he just hoped I'd be equipped, be as skilful as he was, and have enough talents to face the world. He'd given up teaching when he found he could earn a living as a writer—but he'd never really stopped being a teacher. Something, I guessed, Adrian didn't like. I did.

Next day the sun was shining, and though the sea still looked unusually wild and restless, the routines of summer were restored—the swimmers, the families on the beach, the old ladies in the shelters. Dad spent the morning in the garden, tying broken plants to sticks, sweeping up leaves and twigs that the storm had dropped all over the grass and the flower-beds, and grappling with a huge rambling rose that had rambled too much and got itself ripped from a trellis by the wind. "I could give you roots and cuttings to take back to Alresford," he said. "If you'd like them, that is. You told me the garden was a mess—you could do something about that if you wanted to."

"Yes, I do want to. Thanks. I'll . . . have whatever you can spare."

"Well . . . some of that helenium to start with. Lovely colour—yellow as butter. Phlox. Heliopsis. Aubretia, alyssum. Lilies. Not a good time of year to move plants, but if you dig them up carefully, then put them in at once and water them thoroughly, they'll survive. The anemone japonica, the rudbeckia, montbretia . . . those white daisies there, I got them from the churchyard in Wales where my grandfather is buried, and those . . . I don't know what they are, but I call them Edie's Mother's Flowers, because my great-aunt Ethel in Glamorgan was given a bit of it by the mother of her friend Edie, and they're the millionth descendants of that very same root. You ought to have some of it, and the daisies—they're like family heirlooms. But . . . well, I won't dig anything up now; we'll wait till the end of the week."

I hadn't thought of flowers being like family heirlooms, but I suppose you can get fond of a clump of this or a patch of that, just as you feel about any relic or souvenir. "I hope I can carry them all on the train," I said.

"Maybe we could put them in plastic bags and cardboard boxes, and I could drive you home."

"*Drive* me home? Whatever would Mum say if you turned up in Alresford?"

90

He grinned. "She'd get rather a shock, I imagine. Pleasant or unpleasant as the case may be."

"*Will* you?"

He considered that for a while, then muttered "Hmmm . . . ha . . . humph," and turned back to the problem of the rambling rose. "I'll think about it," he said, eventually.

"I'm going indoors to have a glass of water. I'm not sure that . . . I'm feeling too well."

He stopped what he was doing and stared at me. "I thought you were looking pale," he said. "What's the matter?"

"Queasy stomach."

"Last night's apricots?"

"No. They were delicious."

"There's aspirin and paracetemol in the bathroom. You'll find them in the cabinet over the basin."

I lay down on my bed, and stayed there for a couple of hours. It was nothing serious, I was sure; a mild bug I'd picked up in Holland, perhaps—but I didn't feel at all like going for a walk or rushing down to the beach. Dad was now in his study. I could hear the typewriter tapping, somewhat more purposefully than usual. Maybe I was just exhausted—so many new experiences and sensations in such a brief time that my body needed a rest in order to catch up. I dozed. And thought.

All kinds of things I should have thought of before, but which had been crowded out by events. What if the other kids at school knew Dad was gay? I'd become a social leper. As if he was a criminal, a jail-bird; that's what their attitude would be. Or—like father, like son. He is, so I must be. That sort of stupidity. They knew as well as I did that I wasn't, but that would make no difference. I remembered some boy we used to torment because his father owned a fish and chip shop. He smelled, we told him, of stale cooking fat. He didn't, of course, but we spent weeks walking past him holding our noses. Kids can be very cruel. I wouldn't say a word about Dad's sexual orientation, but it was annoying to have to be secretive if I was asked why my parents had split up. His books were all in the school library; people knew I was the author's son and they sometimes questioned me about him. I'd invariably said I knew little and cared less, which was true then—but it would be different now. I felt resentful that Dad's being what he was could force me into telling lies.

The jokes we repeated about homosexuals: not turning your back on them, and don't bend down to pick up something you'd dropped; and they wore women's clothes, minced, lisped, waved their wrists, carried handbags—as if they were female by nature but had been born into the wrong bodies; pouf, poufter, pansy, queer, homo, bender, bent, fairy, faggot, fruit-cake; or they were old men in dirty raincoats who exposed themselves to children in public lavatories and parks. A composite portrait that was grotesque, silly and obviously untrue, but which had its sinister side— evil and predatory. Were there really such people? I hadn't met any, nor come across someone who had. My father wasn't a bit like this. Neither were the three or four boys at school I knew who'd masturbated with each other. Dad may have been different from most fathers—in the way he talked and let me talk about anything under the sun, in preferring men to women for reasons I couldn't understand and probably never would understand—but in every other respect he was an ordinary human being.

He came into my room later with a bowl of soup, and asked how I was. Improving, I said; aspirin seemed to have been all that was necessary. "Do you object to the rude names people like you get called?" I asked.

"Yes, of course. Why?"

"I just wondered. You aren't a bit like . . ."

"The sort of idiot you see on second-rate TV comedy

92

shows? Larry Grayson and John Inman? Of course I'm not. Nor is anybody in real life. Do you think all blacks are violent rapists with neanderthal I.Q.s, that Pakistanis sleep fourteen to a bed, that Jews are evil money-lenders with long Fagin beards? Those are all malicious stereotypes because people are frightened of minority groups."

"Why?" I drank the soup: tomato.

"They see them as threats to the status quo," Dad said, "to a 'normal' way of existence. People don't like what they can't understand. It shouldn't be there, they say. But what *is* normal?"

"Being attracted to the opposite sex, I would have thought."

"And *why* are you attracted to the opposite sex?" he asked.

"I just am. It's . . . normal! There isn't a . . . a *why* to it."

"Roughly ten per cent of the world's population, including me, prefer their own sex. How do you account for that?"

"I . . . I can't. Something . . . must have gone wrong somewhere."

"Nothing went wrong anywhere. There isn't a 'why' to it, as you've just said about yourself fancying girls."

"There must be!"

"Nobody ever asks why men and women are attracted to each other. It's natural, we think, like waking up or smiling or having a pee, and anything different is unnatural. But it isn't so simple. A sizable proportion of the human race is naturally drawn to their own sex. It isn't learned like a foreign language, or unwillingly acquired like a . . . a broken limb. And these men and women aren't freaks—they don't go around wishing they could change their sex. They're not child molesters either, or anything ugly or abnormal you may have heard about from other kids at school.

Many of them are perfectly happy to be what they are, and those who aren't would be just as happy if society didn't continually frown and sneer and tell them they're second-class citizens."

"Here endeth the lesson," I said, and handed him the empty soup bowl. "I just wish . . . *you* weren't."

"Why?"

"It's obvious. I'd have had you all the time, not just for this . . . this little oasis."

"Oasis! That's a good image. Perhaps you'll be a writer, too, one day."

"I wouldn't mind."

"You can't undo the past," he said, and sat down on the end of the bed. "It *is*, as a fact like the present. Let's suppose the past *were* different, and that I wasn't homosexual. My life would not have been the same, oh, from the teenage years onwards. I'd have met lots of girls, probably got married earlier than I did, to—and this is quite likely—someone other than Nora. I *thought* I was heterosexual, but deep down I knew I was different in some . . . some vague, indefinable way. I remember—no, I shouldn't be saying things like this."

"Go on."

"Well . . . I remember the first time a girl allowed me to undo her bra. I thought, so what? What's so interesting about it? When all the other boys were going half-crazy doing that. Or wanting to." It reminded me so much of school now, the boys going half-crazy, etcetera, that I laughed. "You may well laugh!" he went on. "But let's suppose another scenario, a very improbable one. A world where it's possible to be entirely happy growing up gay. Where it isn't regarded as wicked, or unfortunate, or unhealthy. Then I wouldn't have got married at all. Now, what do these two imaginary pasts have in common?"

"Neither would have led to me coming into existence."

"Absolutely right! Would you rather you hadn't been born?"

"No."

"In that case, you have to accept all the complicated circumstances that led up to it."

I sighed. "You tie me up in verbal knots, as usual. You never leave me in a position where I can score a point!"

"Oh, sorry about that!" he said, cheerfully, and drummed a tune on the side of the soup bowl. "Listen . . . I came in here not just to give you soup, but to tell you a couple of things, and I don't remember what they were . . . yes, I do. I've stopped work on that book I'm meant to be finishing; I seem to be quite unable to think of anything worthwhile to put in it. I've started a new story."

"I thought the typewriter was going a bit quicker than usual. What's it about?"

"A teenage boy from a one-parent family goes to stay with his father. He hasn't seen Dad for years, and he discovers that Dad is homosexual."

"Oh. Does it take place in Bournemouth?"

"Some of it will, I guess."

I frowned. I didn't like this at all, though Dad had probably thought I would be flattered. "I wouldn't want anyone at school to read it," I said.

He looked hurt; it was obviously not the reaction he was expecting, nor had the idea occurred to him that I might be bothered if other kids knew the truth. But, as usual, he didn't take long to invent a plausible answer. "By the time it's written," he said, "if it ever gets written and published, and bought by your school library, and that's assuming the librarian would want to buy it and the publisher would want to publish it—we'll both be two years older. At least. You'll be eighteen and just starting, I hope, at a university. You'll have these problems in a different perspective, and you may not care tuppence about what your friends read."

I shrugged my shoulders. "What was the other thing you wanted to tell me?" I asked.

"Oh. Yes." His face brightened. "I'll drive you up to Alresford on Friday."

We set off in his ageing Toyota, the back seat and the boot laden with cardboard boxes full of plants and gardening tools—trowel, fork, shears, secateurs—that he had lent or given to me. This last week had been as good as the rest of this strange holiday—tennis, chess, swimming, and talking about life. We went to Poole, where we explored the harbour and the shops in Old Town; and on another occasion we drove through the New Forest to Lymington for a picnic lunch by the sea. Across the Solent was the Isle of Wight, very different from how it looked at Bournemouth. "I'd like to go there one day," I said.

"I've never been," Dad answered.

"Never? And you live so near!"

"You shouldn't go to some places; you may be disappointed. I think the Isle of Wight has a great deal of mystery. Romance, even. I love staring out of my window at the Needles and the lighthouse, particularly in rough weather. If I go there that could be spoiled. I'm afraid it will be just like anywhere else."

I shook my head. "I don't understand that at all!"

"Who was it said it's better to travel hopefully than to arrive? T.S. Eliot? I can't remember. Have you read Virginia Woolf's *To The Lighthouse*?"

"No."

"James Ramsay, aged six, wants to visit the lighthouse, and is very annoyed because his father won't let him. But he does go eventually, ten years later, and he finds it's just a squat, ugly, functional building covered in bird droppings."

"And the moral is . . . ?"

"Hope deferred maketh the heart sick, I guess."

"I'm Sagittarius. The wanderer."

"Well . . . all I can say is . . . may your lighthouses be beautiful and kindly."

He had travelled, and found Adrian—who was like James Ramsay's lighthouse, perhaps. I had travelled too, and found my father. On the whole, beautiful and kindly: there was, I admit, a certain quantity of bird droppings.

I was thinking of this conversation on the journey to Alresford, and wondering what he would discover when he saw his wife. What *I* would discover: Mum was correct in suggesting I might not be the same person who had left on the train three weeks ago. And what would she make of it all? That similar thoughts were in his mind, I deduced from the words he sang as we sped along the Ringwood by-pass and climbed up to the wild, open heath of the New Forest—

> *Lay that pistol down, ma,*
> *Lay that pistol down;*
> *Pistol-packing momma,*
> *Lay that pistol down!*

As we got nearer to Alresford, passed the signposts to Ovington, then Tichborne, went under the railway bridge and turned into Grange Road, I was surprised to see the accustomed props of my life exactly as I had imagined them. I had shed a skin since I'd been away. I would have to put it back on, or Mum would really be alarmed.

"I think we should go via the station," I said. "They expect me to arrive on the train, and though Mum and Aunt Bridie probably won't come down to meet it, Nic will be there."

He was. And amazed to see me get out of a car, accompanied by a strange man. "This is your Uncle Peter," I said. Nic's expression was absolutely blank.

"My father," I added.

"Oh!" For a brief moment he looked as if he'd met a dangerous alien from outer space, then he said politely "How do you do?"

"I last saw you when you were one month old," Dad said; the three of us giggled with embarrassment, and lapsed into silence.

"We're going up to the house," I said to Nic. "Do you want to come with us?"

"Mmmm . . . thanks . . . but I'm waiting for the three twenty. I might go to Alton in the cab, if Mr Bowles doesn't mind."

"Are Mum and Aunt Bridie at home?"

"They went for a walk by the river, but they shouldn't be long."

Tralee was empty, so I let myself in. "Don't stand on the doorstep," I said to Dad. "Come inside."

"I wonder if I should."

"I'm inviting you."

"Well, in that case . . ." I showed him round, and he told me—I knew it anyway—which were the pieces of furniture he and Mum had owned when they were married, then said Bridie's house hadn't altered a great deal over the years. But what had they done, he asked, with the sideboard, the blue Wilton carpet, the grey sofa, the small wardrobe?

"Mum sold them when we moved in. We didn't need them."

In my bedroom he sat in the peacock chair. "It's ages since I've put my bottom on this," he said. "Nora's re-covered the cushion, I see." He patted the arms, as if he was delighted to say hullo to an old friend. The key turned in the lock downstairs, and I heard Aunt Bridie's voice in the middle of some long story, then Mum say "Yes . . . is that true? . . . I'd never have thought it!" Dad shifted uneasily. "I think I'll stay here for the moment," he said. "You go down and warn them. I don't want Nora to have a heart attack." I protested, but he waved me away; "Get on with it!" he ordered.

It was not the most joyful of family reunions. Aunt Bridie's mouth fell open when I conveyed the news, and she rushed out of the house, probably to inform Mrs Eggins or Mrs Blenkinsop that her ne'er-do-well brother-in-law had breezed in like a bad odour. Mum turned pale, and immediately went upstairs. I followed: I didn't want to miss out on this. Dad was smiling and calm—or at least giving a good imitation of being relaxed; Mum was tense. I had not seen them together for thirteen years! I would have liked to pretend to myself that it was the beginning of a time when he would see a lot more of her, or that he had never been away, was at this moment just dropping in from an office where he worked to say he'd be home early for dinner. But that would have been daft. Childish.

Dad explained about the plants and how I couldn't have carried them all on the train, and said that he did not intend to stop long, but it would have been rude just to leave without a word. Mum said she was surprised to hear I was interested in gardening, but, well, a splash of colour outside wouldn't do anyone any harm. It was a stiff, polite conversation at first—the sort two acquaintances have while waiting for a bus that is overdue, neither of them really interested in what is being said, as their minds are more concerned with what will happen when they arrive late for their appointments. Mum asked a few questions about Amsterdam, and whether Dad was writing anything at the moment, and she hoped I hadn't been a nuisance; he asked how Aunt Bridie was, talked about the weather, and said that the tourist season in Bournemouth was much the same as usual.

Then, as if he considered these topics a waste of time,

Dad said "We should see each other more often. There's no good reason why not."

"Well . . . yes . . ." Mum answered, and nervously cracked the joints of her fingers.

"We should have been able to stay friends. Many people do."

"Peter . . . Michael's here."

"He doesn't need protection. He's not a child any longer."

Mum's face hardened. "That's for me to judge," she snapped.

"You ought to come down to Bournemouth and stay for a day or two."

"I . . . I don't quite know what I'd find there."

Dad was obviously angered by this remark, but he continued to talk in the same soft, reasonable tone of voice. "Nothing that would offend your maiden aunt," he said.

Mum stared down at her lap, and brushed away some invisible specks of dirt. "That part of my life is finished. I don't want to dig up painful memories . . . open old wounds. Every link is broken, and it's just as well they are."

"Not true," Dad said. "There's Mike."

"What about him?"

"Links."

"For years he's not even troubled his head with thoughts of his father. It was as if you didn't exist. And he was perfectly happy. Then you had to ring up that night and change it all!" She sounded very resentful.

"Why did you let him come?"

"Yes," I said, butting into the conversation. "Why did you let me?"

My mother turned to me. "You've probably discovered this past three weeks how very nice and convincing and persuasive your father can be. He has a reply to everything, and in any argument or discussion he leaves you without a leg to stand on. Yes, even on the telephone! You end up driven into silence, or else forced to agree with him. You agree, for the sake of a quiet life. I'd been on the Guinness, and—"

"Doing the Lambeth Walk," I said.

"—and my powers of reasoning weren't up to their usual standard. Not that they match his when they are!" She moved to the door. "Would you like a drink, Peter, before you go?"

"Ah . . . hmmm . . . yes, please," Dad said.

We went downstairs and drank some dry sherry. Aunt Bridie was still out. "Why can't you be friends?" I asked. "Why go on having a grudge all these years?" The sherry, I guess, was loosening my tongue.

They both looked embarrassed. "In *my* book," Mum said, "a promise is a promise, particularly those you make in the marriage vows. To have and to hold . . . for better for worse . . . till death do us part. They're not like paper chains, broken three days after Christmas."

"But you forced him to leave!"

"Oh, he told you that, did he?"

"Mike," Dad said sternly, "drop the subject!"

"I've decided something," I said. "And it's very important. During the school holidays, from now on, I'm going to live in Bournemouth."

Mum put her glass down on the table with such a sweeping gesture its stem broke. She walked out of the room, then out of the house.

"If you'll have me," I said to Dad.

"Je-sus." He took a deep breath. "You certainly know the mechanics of how to create a grand scene! Of course you can come to Bournemouth, whenever you wish. Though . . . I don't think for one moment that Nora will let you." But he looked hugely pleased, like a kid who'd just discovered an unopened birthday present that had been forgotten.

"If I really want to," I said, "I don't see that she can stop me."

"Yes . . . well . . . you'll have to work on that. Now . . . I think I'd better be going."

A few minutes later the red Toyota was disappearing into the distance.

7. Embracing the world

Shunting practice. The trucks were clonk-clonk-clonk-clonking into each other, and the ancient, arthritic engine was wheezing and whiffling, on the whole sounding as if it were pleased with its performance. *Roma Termini* and *Conseil Supérieur de Chemins de Fer* were gliding to a gentle halt on track number two. Beyond the railway embankment the river wound as lazily as always between the flat water meadows, its willows weeping and its weeds awash in the current. Pillars of gnats danced. A kingfisher flashed. Nothing had changed, and everything had changed.

But I tried to show for Nic's benefit that it hadn't. I squatted beside him on the embankment, our faces inches from the engine's great iron wheels, and I thought how boring it all was compared with flying in aeroplanes, eating in Indonesian restaurants, and talking adult-to-adult. "Did that boy ever show up again?" I asked.

"What boy?"

"Sid something-or-other."

"I found out he lives in Bishop's Sutton."

"He hasn't bothered you when you've been camping at the fulling mill?"

"Haven't seen him at all," Nic said, swishing at a fly that was trying for the third time to settle on his nose.

"How did you work that? Sleeping at the mill?"

"I waited till they were on the Guinness. Mum got stung by a bee that afternoon and needed a little drop, she said, to take her mind off the pain. Aunt Nora had to dance the Lambeth Walk by herself."

"What else is new, while I've been away?"

"Nothing." Shunting had evidently finished; Mr Bowles, holding an oil can, climbed down from the engine and trudged along the track to the station. We stood up, and ran down the embankment to the path by the river. "Someone's buried a dead dog," Nic said. "Just beyond the fulling mill. There's a little wooden cross on the grave, with 'Fido ever faithful' carved on it, and the dates. Why should anyone want to do that?"

"No idea."

"Would you like to see it?"

"Not particularly."

The path took us over a bridge where a gurgling exuberant rivulet joined the main stream. Nic kneeled, as he often did here, and trailed his arms in the water. Wild cress grew on the stream's bed, and he pulled some of it up. "Ever tried this stuff?" he asked.

"No."

"It tastes revolting." He ate it. "Like iron. Like chewing an engine wheel." He spat it out. "Must have been nice, staying with your dad. You know, when I do things I'm pleased about, like finding an easier way than you did of climbing into the fulling mill, I think, oh, I must tell Dad when he gets home, and then I know I can't because he's dead. It isn't . . . fair, somehow."

"I read in some book that fairness is a word invented by adults to keep children quiet." He had seen himself and me, despite the difference in our ages, as having a kind of equality being without fathers; now that had been taken from him. "Next time I go there," I said, "perhaps you can come with me. He is your uncle."

"Could I?" His eyes lit up. "I think I might enjoy that. Is there a station?"

"Yes. But it's an ordinary sort of station, not a bit like Alresford. It's called Pokesdown."

"Pokesdown!" He laughed. "What else is there? What's in the house?"

"A harp. I want to learn how to play it."

"Does it belong to the man from the Wessex Philharmonic Symphony?"

"Yes."

"I don't suppose Mum would let me go," he said, rather wistfully. "She doesn't approve of Uncle Peter. Is he . . . bad, or something?"

"No. He's not bad. Not bad at all."

"I like the garden you've made."

I had already spent several back-breaking hours pulling up weeds, preparing the soil, digging the plants in and watering them: two bits of the wilderness, on each side of the house, now looked quite respectable. One I christened the summer gardens, as I had given the phlox, montbretia, rudbeckia, heleniums and so on their homes there; the other one was the winter gardens—for chrysanthemums, yellow jasmine, kaffir lilies and snowdrop bulbs. Aunt Bridie asked why I didn't mix the two together so we could have something in bloom in the same flower-bed the whole year round. I told her I liked the idea of keeping them separate, and she said she supposed it wasn't her affair; I could do as I wished as I was putting in all the hard work.

We had reached the fulling mill, and I was intrigued to know how Nic had discovered an easier way of getting in than I had done. He took me to an outhouse, a sort of shed attached to the side of the mill, opened the door and dragged out an old, worm-eaten step-ladder, no bigger than himself but obviously ideal for climbing from the top of the water-butt to the chimney.

"I never thought of looking in there!" I said, admiringly.

"You have to have brains," Nic answered. "The only trouble is, when I've got to the chimney, I like to pull the ladder up after me in case anyone sees it and tries to get in. Rather an effort, heaving it up on to the roof."

Between us, it was no effort at all and in next to no time

we were down the chimney and inside the mill.

He had turned it into a second home. His sleeping-bag was there—on an air-bed—and cushions, books, crockery, cutlery, a primus stove, a kettle, tea, milk, sugar, a tin full of cakes, a flashlight and a bucket. "Where did all this stuff come from?" I asked.

"Tralee," he said. "They don't seem to have missed any of it. Yet."

"What do you do if it rains?"

"It hasn't so far. But it could be a problem, as the chimney's open to the sky. Will you sleep here tonight? I've been really looking forward to you coming home so we can both camp out in this place! I was extremely disappointed when you rang up and said you were staying another week."

"O.K." It was the last thing I wanted to do, sleeping in a damp, sooty, ruined mill. But I didn't want to hurt Nic. Even a partial wriggling back into the uncomfortably tight old skin of childhood was not easy.

"What I don't understand," I said, "is why you thought it necessary to protect me so much. I've been starved of information all these years! I didn't know what the answers were, because I . . . I didn't know the questions!"

"I was afraid he would take you away from me. He seems to have been successful." Mum looked very small and bleak. Aunt Bridie was in the kitchen, noisily washing up. Nic was at the fulling mill.

This deflated my anger: it was the truth. The honest truth; I felt that instinctively. She didn't mean take me away by force, the kind of drama you sometimes read about in the newspapers—Man Kidnaps Son—but 'take' in a more subtle sense of the word. She meant his disarming, attractive personality, his . . . his charisma would seduce me into feeling life with him was a lot more exciting than the dullness of Tralee. Or that he would give a tremendous display of that side of his character while I was in Bournemouth so I would be impressed. But I hadn't been deceived by someone putting on an act; everything about him was genuine. I think.

"I'm here," I said. "And I . . . I shan't go to Bournemouth till . . . I don't know . . . Christmas perhaps. If he invites me."

"Christmas!" She looked alarmed and hurt at the idea of her only son not being with her at Christmas.

"Well . . . maybe not Christmas itself. New Year. As for living with him permanently, I don't want to. And I don't suppose he'd like it, either. He probably *would* think that was rather a nuisance."

"As always," Mum said bitterly, "he pursues his pleasures and evades his responsibilities."

"He sends us money every month."

"He has to. By order of the Divorce Court."

"O.K. . . . ." I was exasperated; conversations like this went along parallel lines that never met. Mum was the most rigid parallel line I knew of. "What do you feel he should do?"

She didn't answer that, but said after a moment's pause "Was there anybody else in the house, living there?"

"A friend of his. Adrian."

"Friend?"

"Lover." The word made her wince, as if she had been stung. "He left. For good."

"The Wessex harpist, I presume."

She sounded as if she'd like to hear the details, but I didn't particularly want to launch into an analysis of that furore; to do so would be a kind of betrayal. It wasn't my business, and it certainly wasn't hers. I was not going to act as a spy on my parents' lives, regaling each of them with bits of gossip about the other. But I did say "He's now the harpist of the Mersey Philharmonic."

"Oh. How did Peter react to that?"

"He's all right."

She guessed that I would not say any more, I think, for she stood up as if to signal that our chat was over; but I was on the point of leaving the room when she said "I hope you aren't in any way . . . like he is."

This was the first time my mother had ever made any reference, oblique or otherwise, to the fact that she was aware of me as a sexual being. "It isn't hereditary," I said.

"Probably not," she agreed. "But people can be . . . dangerous influences."

"I like girls," I said, looking at her straight in the eye. I wasn't tempted to do so, but it did occur to me that if I told her what had happened in Amsterdam she would be reassured on that point. Shocked, upset, maybe outraged . . . but reassured.

"Do you have a girlfriend?" she asked.

"No."

"Then how can you be certain?"

I laughed. "I'm certain!"

"Well . . ." She sighed. "Maybe there's nothing to worry about. But I wish people like your father could decide who they are and what they are before they begin ruining other people's existences."

"I guess he wishes the same thing. Wishes those like himself could be allowed to make their minds up sooner than he was able to."

"Most of them do nowadays. And nobody's prohibiting the others."

"Aren't they? You wouldn't be thrilled if I was gay— you implied that just now. You couldn't stop me, in a literal sense . . . but wouldn't you, and the rest of the world, make me feel guilty—or dirty, or evil? So that I'd try not to be gay, as I imagine Dad felt he was forced to do."

"You know too much for your own good, in my opinion," Mum said. "Too clever by half. You have the same ability as your father has to make black sound like white. To mess about with words so nobody else can argue. It isn't that marvellous a gift—you can end up smug and conceited."

"Or a writer. That would be . . . oh, great!"

"Get out of here and let me do the cleaning! I want to dust this room and hoover the carpet."

Aunt Bridie came in, so absolutely on cue, it seemed, that I wondered if she had been listening at the key-hole—I hadn't heard the sounds of crockery being washed for the last five minutes. She looked at my mother, as if she expected her to say something, but Mum was busy feather-dusting the lampshades. "Every-thing all right in here?" she asked.

"What do you imagine is wrong?" I answered.

"Wrong?" Aunt Bridie echoed. "There's a great deal wrong with the world, Michael. You don't need me to tell you that. Nuclear weapons and greedy unions, Russians and the price of everything these days, and good men dying before they should and bad men running away from their responsibilities, and children not showing any gratitude to mothers who've brought them up single-handed."

"You're bitter, frustrated, and sex-starved!" I shouted, then ran out of the room, slamming the door. Why did I say that, I asked myself, true though it was. It would mean trouble. A lot of trouble. But as I left the house, I heard, to my surprise, Mum not expressing sympathy for her sister, but demanding angrily why Bridie always had to put her foot in it, particularly when it was something really delicate to do with me.

I walked down the road, under the railway bridge, up Station Approach and past the church. The church was old—bits of it Saxon — but it wasn't all that interesting, nor was the green around it, which was excessively tidy, the tombstones removed from their original places and set along the walls in order to make life easier for the man who mowed the grass. It wasn't somewhere you could experience the kind of feelings you normally did in graveyards—profound, or melancholy, or poetic—just a short cut through to the busy High Street. Here, despite the traffic—it was the A31, the main road from Alton to Winchester—was a better sense of the past than by the church. The Swan Hotel and the Bell Hotel stood on opposite sides of the street, coaching inns that had changed very little in their appearance since the eighteenth century. I knew the names of all the Alresford pubs, though I had never been in one. I could see, from where I was standing, the Running Horses up the other side of the big dip where the A31 zoomed down to the Cheriton cross-roads; best beer in Alresford, my uncle had often said. Out of sight were the Peaceful Home, the Globe, the Horse and Groom and the Cricketers' Arms. (The latter, about a mile out of town by the golf course, was where my uncle drank many a week-end lunch.) There used to be the Sun, the Volunteer's Arms and the Dean Arms, but these establishments, ages ago, had been sold off and turned into private houses. Every building in this street was old, and you could see where Alresford finished, abruptly, as if there was an agreed point where the countryside should start. There was no twentieth century glass and concrete at either end of the town, no gradual thinning out of houses, or that dreary mixture you see so often of petrol stations, car dumps, and derelict fields. It was as if for generations people here had said the countryside was not to be raped.

Yes, there were changes, like the Sun and the Volunteer's Arms no longer being pubs. The china shop where Aunt Bridie had once bought a bowl was now a café. The coffee shop Mum would often take me to when I was little now sold clothes, and its owner, peg-leg Lilian, with her Hampshire burr so pronounced you could hardly understand what she was talking about, was dead and under the churchyard grass. The two-roomed infants' school I went to when I was five was now a store-place for a builder's merchant. But these alterations did not affect the face of the town: nothing here *seemed* to be different. Welches' fish shop was exactly as it had always been. When I was seven or eight, Marigold Welch was my girlfriend. There was a disused chicken-house at the bottom of her garden, but no chickens, which had long since been eaten for Sunday dinners. Marigold and I often sat in it and kissed. On more than one occasion we undressed each other completely. Her mother caught us once, and said she would tell my mother. I waited in fear and trembling, but nothing happened. Mrs Welch, presumably, considered it was not so awful a deed as Mum would have thought, and decided not to bother with traipsing up to Tralee to tell her story. I wondered if Marigold might be as interested in what my body was like now as I would be in hers, and I peered through the fish shop window. But she wasn't there.

I walked along Broad Street, and took the path by the watercress beds to the fulling mill. I shouted for Nic, but there was no answer; so I clambered on to the roof and yelled "Nic!" down the chimney. Silence. If I followed the river I would find myself back by the railway station and home: I didn't want to return. Instead, I struck out across the fields, uphill, away from the placid willows and poplars, the huddling town, and on to the chalk hills with their wide, sweeping views, lolloping hares and larks singing like dribbling taps. Up here you feel free. The white, dusty path led to Abbotstone, a village—a hamlet, no more than a collection of farms—I'd never been to before.

I should never have shouted at my aunt. It was awful! I would apologise, whether Mum insisted or not.

But my coments were right, I was certain, and they applied with equal truth to Mum herself. The two sisters, because something dreadful had happened to them both, had in a sense stopped living; they'd shrivelled. Withered. Even if they had their moments of fun, and continued to care about their children, they had lost . . . what was it? Tolerance. The ability to leap into new situations. A love of life. Dad hadn't. Nothing would make him stop living, not Adrian's departure, a succession of books that didn't sell, or the fear of loneliness. His battle, I guess, was long ago, the one in which he finally accepted himself for what he was; a battle he had won, and no problem that occurred subsequently had forced him to bow his head and surrender.

I would be like him, not like Mum. I want to go on struggling against whatever it may be that could threaten my whole existence, and when I'm carried out in my coffin at the age of ninety-two I'll still be screaming.

I want to travel the whole wide world, and write lots of books. Meet scores of women. Get married one day, and have children I'll attempt to understand and talk to. Leave Alresford as soon as I'm grown up. See Dad, often. More immediately, I want to improve my tennis, find myself a girlfriend, and learn how to play that harp.

These lofty thoughts and resolutions flew out of my head when I rounded a corner of the hills and saw Abbotstone. So that's what it's like, I said to myself. Nothing special. A few old cottages buried in fields. The only humans there, as far as I could tell, were two ancient farm labourers who stopped chatting as I passed in order to stare at me very suspiciously. Several dogs barked as I walked on, but that was all. Soon I was up the other side of the hill, over the top, and Abbotstone was out of sight. Like the mad boy, it seemed to be a piece of another life, a figment of a dream.

I went as far as Itchen Abbas, and came home on the three twenty train—in the cab with Mr Bowles. "Long time since you've done this!" he shouted over the roar of the engine, and I nodded.

Chuffa-chuffa, chuffa-chuffa, chuffa-chuffa. Cows swishing their tails in damp meadows on either side of the railway, the river here flat and sluggish, now there purposeful and swift; dark patches on its surface indicating luxuriant growth of weed or reed underneath; dazzling patches glittering in the sun like light on pewter. The best place, over there, in April for kingcups. Jam jars and tiddlers: once I'd got saturated and plastered with mud, and was given the inevitable lecture when I returned to Tralee. The engine's smoke, fleecy white clouds evaporating above the fields. Now the bridge over the A31 and the water research station where my uncle used to be boss; the land rising sharply so that we were now in the cutting. Smoke everywhere, and it wasn't possible to see much, only a sprawl of stinging nettles and rosebay willow herb, a shed, a woman at the end of her garden grabbing sooty washing from a line; then out into the sun and Mrs Tope's trees which would soon have their red September crop of plastic balls, the sidings, the trucks, *Roma Termini*: Alresford Station. The creaks and groans as the sinews of the old train braced themselves to stop. Goodbye and thanks to Mr Bowles for the trip. Nic on the platform, grinning, pleased and surprised to see me. The slamming of doors; Colonel Ramsbottom home from work. Home is the sailor, home from sea.

Plus ça change, plus c'est la même chose.

That was all a long time ago, five years; I'm twenty-one now and I graduated this summer from the University of Cambridge with a first-class honours degree in English. I'm living in North London—I've been here four months—in a house with my girlfriend and a dozen other young people, though at week-ends the influx of visitors makes it seem like two dozen young people. Some of us work; some of us are unemployed. I'm one of the lucky ones—I've recently started at the foot of the ladder in a publishing consortium. It won't make me rich very quickly, but it's what I decided, some while ago, I wanted to do to earn my living, for, if I just sat in my room and wrote books, I would starve to death. I like the job. And I'm writing. I began to write in my first term at Cambridge—short stories and poems, a few of which appeared in student magazines. Now this . . . this novel, or autobiographical fragment, is almost finished. Whether anyone will care to publish it, let alone read it, is totally beyond prediction. But I shall send it off and wait for the rejection slips, or for what would be the happiest day of my life—a letter in the mail which says, yes, we'll take it.

Only Dad has seen the manuscript—no-one else, not even my beautiful, attractive, lovable girlfriend. Dad said the "I" of the book was undoubtedly an accurate self-portrait—arrogant, over-confident and sex-crazy; but he was very non-committal about my chances of seeing the thing in print. (Though he obviously enjoyed it. He would, wouldn't he? He comes out of it rather well.) "Who's it *for*?" he asked.

"For? Anyone who wants to read it, as you once said yourself about your own books."

"But you must have some sort of market in mind," he said, impatiently. "Is it a novel for young adults?"

"I don't know. Yes. I suppose so."

"In that case, you'll have to cut out the swearing. And the sex. Also, I don't think people will believe a sixteen-year-old from a sleepy country town, however bright and intelligent, thinks and feels as maturely as your narrator."

I capitulated on the first two points, though a great many adolescents know about four-letter words and use them as often as their parents do. I argued that there was almost no sex, and it would be dishonest in a book with a boy of that age telling the story to leave it out altogether. True, Dad replied, but try saying that to the Moral Majority. The last point I defended passionately—I was recording exactly what I thought and felt and how I spoke at that time, and if it was more mature than the behaviour of an average kid I couldn't help that. Adults, I said, *never* realize where teenagers have arrived; they invariably imagine kids will be younger than they actually are, as if they didn't somehow want their children to grow up, or were frightened of them doing so. Dad agreed, but suggested I was nevertheless bringing later experience to bear on my sixteen-year-old life; memory distorts, he said: it selects. One always rewrites history. No, no, no! I cried. That summer was recorded in my head in detail as vivid as you'd see in a photograph.

He still lives in the Bournemouth house, alone. He has had a few relationships since Adrian left, but nothing serious. He doesn't want anything serious, no binding promises, till-death-do-us-part stuff. It would interfere with his work, he says, and he seems to be in quite a productive phase, two novels a year, though he never got round to doing the book about the three weeks in which he re-discovered his son—which is why I've done it for him. He may be alone, but he isn't lonely. There is usually someone somewhere. He's fifty, but I guess he's still an attractive man because he has energy. Energy is eternal delight, William Blake said.

I, too, at this stage of my life, don't want a relationship with binding promises, though Dad says that's because I'm an archetypal male chauvinst pig. I say I'm too young to be married—there is so much to do, to experience first. Kids who are hitched at twenty and think they're settling down to a life just like their parents', with washing-machines and mortgages and nappies, are out of their tiny minds. They usually end up in the divorce courts when they're twenty-five. I do, however, hope I'll get married and have children—a long time off in the distant future. In my thirties. I want to be sure that it will work, for one thing I'm determined on is *not* to end up in the divorce courts. I know from my own childhood and teenage years how dreadful that can be.

I did go to Bournemouth for much of my holiday time when I was seventeen and eighteen, and one summer Nic went with me. I think Mum and Aunt Bridie gradually—if grudgingly—admitted to themselves that being with my father didn't corrupt me, and that it was therefore all right for Nic. He enjoyed himself very much, I seem to remember. He's seventeen now, and madly in love with Marigold Welch's sister, Morella.

Aunt Bridie still lives at windy Tralee, and I don't think anything that happens in the future will change that, or her. But you never know: the big astonishment of the past five years is that Mum was introduced to a man, married him, and moved out to live in Basingstoke. I don't see her as often as I see Dad, though I occasionally go down to their bungalow for a week-end, which, I have to confess, I find pretty tedious. I just don't have a lot to say to Mum or to Kevin. Nor they to me, and I suspect Mum doesn't really care for anything I do, my values, my way of life. With one very obvious difference, I'm too much like my father. But she's happy, which pleases and re-assures me, a lot happier than during all those years she lived with her sister. She taught Kevin how to do the Lambeth Walk, and once a week they go to some club, do old-time dancing and drink Guinness.

As for those ambitions I outlined the day I went to Abbotstone, some of them I achieved, some I did not. The improvement in my tennis is marginal and my chess is a little rusty, though when I'm with Dad some of his love for both games is contagious and rubs off on me. I didn't learn to play the harp, alas. Adrian appeared one morning about six months after he'd left and removed it. I don't think Dad ever saw him again, and I'm pretty certain they haven't been writing letters. What I have achieved is the will (I don't know about the ability) to write, and I've indulged my Sagittarian taste for wandering. I haven't revisited Amsterdam, but the week I spent there with Dad really whetted my appetite for foreign travel, and I'm hoping—if I can afford it—to fly with my girlfriend to San Francisco next year. Dad said he may come with us.

She's Brazilian, and very musical. Last week she persuaded me—I was reluctant at first—to go with her to the Festival Hall where the Wessex Philharmonic Symphony was performing, believe it or not, Mahler's tenth. The harpist, of course, was no longer a curly-haired young blond man, but a severe-looking middle-aged female with scarlet lips and Mary Whitehouse spectacles. I knew my reactions would not be the same; I was much older, a different person—but I was surprised at *how* different my feelings were. This was not, I realized, the final creation of a man looking at all the superb sunsets that had gone for ever; certainly it was bitter-sweet, but it was also robust and life-enhancing. The soaring tune in the first movement brought back vividly that night in Bournemouth: the Winter Gardens and a young harpist plucking the strings, eyes intent on the conductor, my father beside me totally involved, his eyes just as intent, but fixed on the man and the instrument producing those exquisite sounds. Not death that music, but a vision of the ideal, and a knowledge that the ideal is an illusion.

I haven't been to Alresford for years, but I don't suppose it's changed. Marigold Welch and I did go out for about six months—and it was very different from my relationship with Miranda. It began a few days after my walk to Abbotstone, but I'm not going to rake it all up now: this book isn't written for a bunch of peeping toms. Maybe Dad's right about me being a male chauvinist pig. She also said I was; I only wanted her for her body was her verdict, and it had been a mistake on her part to allow it.

The railway, as far as I know, is still there, and Mr Bowles, the shunting practices, and Colonel Rams-bottom, if he isn't retired or dead, commuting to work. I have to confess that my childish enthusiasm for railways endures. I enjoy studying maps and timetables, and I read books about trains. When *Great Train Journeys of the World* was shown on TV I was glued to the set every Wednesday night. But Alton, Medstead and Four Marks, Ropley, Alresford, Itchen Abbas and Winchester, though they may have once been as exotic to me as Chimborazo, Cotopaxi and Popocatépetl, don't steal my heart nowadays; I plan—if I'm ever rich enough—to travel from Sydney across the Nullarbor Plain to Perth, from London to Venice on the Orient Express, from New York to Los Angeles on the California Zephyr. In the programme at last week's concert, Mahler was quoted as saying "My symphonies embrace everything, like the world." I like that, as an ambition: I'm going to embrace the world, too.

I expect, now I've left Alresford, that the flowers I planted there have vanished under the weeds. One day I'm going to have a garden of my own—a dazzling riot of blossom. And no messing about with seasonal flower-beds; Aunt Bridie was right—there should be bloom all the year round.

One good reason for that is I'm sure Mum, Dad and I came out of the winter gardens long ago and left them far behind us.